A WORD TO THE WITCH

AN EIRA SNOW COZY MYSTERY (BOOK TWO)

Victoria DeLuis

For J.

With special thanks to my family and Aimee.

Published in 2021 by
Deryn Publishing
United Kingdom

First Edition

© 2021 Victoria DeLuis @ Deryn Publishing
www.victoriadeluis.com

All characters, places and events are fictional. Any resemblance to real persons, places or events is purely coincidental.

The moral rights of the author have been asserted.

All rights reserved. No part of this publication may be reproduced, copied, stored or distributed in any form, without prior written permission of the publisher.

CONTENTS

Chapter One	1
Chapter Two	10
Chapter Three	16
Chapter Four	22
Chapter Five	29
Chapter Six	37
Chapter Seven	46
Chapter Eight	54
Chapter Nine	61
Chapter Ten	66
Chapter Eleven	75
Chapter Twelve	83
Chapter Thirteen	89
Chapter Fourteen	96
Chapter Fifteen	100
Chapter Sixteen	106
Chapter Seventeen	113
Chapter Eighteen	117
Chapter Nineteen	120
Chapter Twenty	128

CHAPTER ONE

My hair puffed up around my head like a cotton ball and trailed down over my shoulder in great waves of dark brown. I huffed out a deep breath and stared at my reflection, lamenting my lack of products.

When Susan had suggested we accompany Gemma to her baking competition and make an event of the entire weekend by booking into the Celtic Manor hotel, I'd jumped at the chance, especially when I heard we'd have time to enjoy the spa. What did it matter that we all lived less than five minutes away? A break was a break, and I hadn't taken one since moving to Caerleon a few months ago. I deserved a little downtime.

"That's right." I gave a firm nod to my reflection. "You most certainly do." After solving a murder, relaunching the store, and training my apprentice, Fleur, I hadn't had time for a break, and I was determined to enjoy myself.

I sighed and slumped my shoulders, surveying the disaster that was my hair once again. I was due to meet Susan and Gemma in the bar in ten minutes. I had nowhere near enough time to pop home and grab some product. I still couldn't believe I'd failed to pack any. They should have been the first things in my bag. Although... I could always pop down to the hotel salon and see if they had anything that would make me look vaguely presentable. But given that it was almost 8 pm, I doubted they'd be open. No. There was nothing to do but tie it back. I delved into my bag, retrieved a hair tie and some pins, and decided to wrestle my unruly mane into a French plait. After a while, and a fair bit of cursing, I managed to create a plait/bun combo that didn't look too bad at all.

I glanced at the clock on the wall and noted I was running late. With one final check in the mirror, I surveyed my teeth for lipstick and, finding none, smoothed down the skirt of my tea-length pleated dress before grabbing my bag and heading out the door.

My pulse raced. I had to admit that I was more than a little nervous as I paced along the corridor. The lush deep-blue carpet muffled my steps and made my heartbeat all the more noticeable. I smiled at a young couple as they passed and hoped it wasn't as obvious to them as it was to me.

Susan and Gemma were both new friends of mine, and I wanted more than anything for the weekend to go well. I couldn't remember a time in my life when I'd actually had 'girl-friends' or people I could go out and just have fun with. Susan, I'd met whilst investigating her friend Tanya's murder, and although I'd seen Gemma many times at her café, we'd become a lot closer after she and her daughter attended the reopening party for my store, Crystal Magic.

Susan met Gemma when I dragged her to the café for some much-needed sustenance after we'd enjoyed a movie and an abundance of vodka one night at her place. They'd hit it off immediately. It was Susan who persuaded Gemma to enter the baking competition. She'd become a firm favourite of Gemma's cooking after declaring her *mille-feuille* the best she had ever tasted. As soon as Gemma learned that was just posh for a cream slice, she was over the moon, although still a little reluctant to enter any competitions. Needless to say, we both soon learned how determined and persuasive Susan could be when she set her mind to something.

We'd arrived at the hotel and checked in at around two. After ensuring everything was set up for Gemma tomorrow and discovering when and where she needed to report, we'd spent some time in the pool and then indulged in a massage as well as both a manicure and pedicure. We were all utterly relaxed afterwards and decided to grab a little shuteye before meeting up in the reception before heading to the court bar.

I pressed the button for the elevator and waited for a few seconds, watching the light signalling where it was going. When I saw it highlight the floor below mine and then descend again, I tapped the button five more times and pulled my phone from my purse.

"Fleur," I said as soon as she answered. "I just wanted to make sure everything was all right."

"Relax and enjoy yourself," she said. "Everything's fine. Niles is making sure of that."

I smiled at the edge to her voice. At twenty, Fleur had come late to magic. Most start training from the moment they are born and have a familiar bonded to them by their first birthday. Niles was my familiar. Abby, a little white floofball with a black puffy tail, had become Fleur's. But in much the same way Fleur was coming late to the game, so too was Abby, and to say that the cat had shown herself to be a little... shall we say, feisty with her newfound powers would be an understatement. I'd been reluctant to leave Fleur alone with her, even for the weekend. When she reassured me that between her and Niles, they could stop Abby from turning into a leopard and terrorising the neighbours, I'd relented. I was only five minutes away if needed, after all, and have I mentioned how much in need of a break I was?

"Call if you need me," I said and winced, dragging the phone away from my ear as Fleur bellowed at Abby to drop the sofa *this instant*. A loud thud followed. Remarkable strength was another of Abby's powers that she seemed to delight in. Last week, when

Fleur made the mistake of closing the door when she took a bath, the rascal swiped it from its hinges.

"Eira, we'll be fine," Fleur said, returning her attention to our call.

"Just remember the exercises I taught you. If you keep her busy, I'm sure she'll stay entertained and out of trouble."

Fleur chuckled. "Niles has sat on her for the moment, and she seems pretty content to let him. I'll let them play for a while and try the exercises again later."

"Sounds like a plan." The lift pinged, and the doors opened in front of me. "I've got to go. Don't forget to cal—"

"I know. I know. I'll call if I need you. Now go. Have fun."

I laughed, ended the conversation, and stepped inside the lift. It was good to have an apprentice, but even better to find a true friend in Fleur, even if she was half my age. It was shocking how quickly she'd become an essential part of my life. If things had been different with Abby, she'd be here now, enjoying the evening with us.

The ornate doors of the lift opened onto the opulent reception area, and the sound of chatter reached my ears. With the muffling carpet a thing of the past, I became conscious of the clop of my heels on the tiled floor. I cleared my throat and tried not to fidget, convinced that everyone must be looking at me. I felt so out of place in the five-star resort. Susan informing me that she had once run into Johnny Depp in the restaurant way back in 2004 didn't help. Nor the fact that world leaders, including then-President Barack Obama, had visited in 2014 for a NATO Summit. Not to mention members of the royal family.

Mustering my courage, I glanced around but couldn't spot Susan or Gemma anywhere. I pulled my phone from my bag to check the time: 8:07 pm. I sighed and shook my head. I should have known that out of the three of us, I'd be the one closest to being on time. I walked to the circular lounge area in the middle of the reception and sat in a rich burgundy armchair that gave me a good view of both the lift and the doors to the outside. I smiled and sniffed at the vase of sunflowers in the middle of the accompanying coffee table before shifting the cushion behind my back to make myself more comfortable. A man in beige trousers and a baby blue shirt sat a few clusters over, engrossed with his phone. He must have felt my gaze as he lifted his head and nodded. His accompanying smile was warm and friendly, so I smiled back. Even though he returned his attention to his phone, his demeanour made me relax a little. Maybe I didn't look as out of place as I felt.

The entrance to the lobby banged open, and an army of footsteps stomped the floor. I turned my attention to the commotion. A man had burst through the doors. Despite the ruckus that came with his appearance, he exuded a sense of calm and power. An entourage accompanied him, although security may be the more appropriate term. Four men flanked him, two on either side, all wearing the same black suits and skinny ties. I'd place them in their late twenties or early thirties, a good decade or two younger than the man they surrounded. They looked more than capable of military-style operations.

My head popped up. Even beneath the dark sunglasses and Panama hat, I recognised the man as Jeremy Dancer. I'd always admired the blend of muted gold and brown of his hair, which shone like the Bruno Jasper stone. He wore it twisted in his signature bun.

This had to be the first time I'd been close to a real live celebrity, and although I wasn't normally one to swoon and fawn over such characters, my heart raced. Susan had mentioned the celebrity chef was one of the judges, but I imagined seeing him sat on a dais, lording over everyone and passing down judgement, not walking within ten feet of me. I found myself standing to get a better view, but blushed when the action caused him to notice me. He smiled and removed his sunglasses. My blush deepened.

He froze, his gaze never leaving my own. His mouth opened as if he was about to say something, and I wondered if I had a pen and paper in my purse should he ask if I wanted an autograph. Not that I did. It just felt rude of me not to be prepared should he offer.

A shrill call spared me embarrassment. All eyes rushed to

the young woman in her mid-twenties who entered with an entourage of her own. She repeatedly shrieked Dancer's name and berated him for leaving her in the car, while flicking her long hair over her shoulder. An act all the more noticeable as her hair happened to be pink. I tried to place a stone or crystal that it most closely matched and couldn't. Rhodonite might come close, but I think bubble-gum-pink was a more apt description. The chef instantly deflated. All his confidence seemed to flee him in an instant. He turned to the woman in the sleek black dress and lifted his arms in mock surrender.

"I merely wanted to check in and gain our room key without the need for you to loiter in the foyer," he said in soothing tones.

The woman huffed and crossed her arms. She did not look even slightly pleased. "You've dragged me to this God-forsaken place. The least you could do was help me out of the car with my things."

I raised an eyebrow and sat back down in my chair, witnessing a domestic wasn't on my to-do list this weekend. Still, I couldn't help overhearing the exasperation in Jeremy Dancer's voice when he mentioned how he'd told her many times that she was more than welcome to stay home and that it was only by her insistence that she'd accompanied him.

She instantly turned on the waterworks, stamping her foot and blubbering like a two-year-old whose parents refused to let them eat a whole tub of ice-cream. She stepped closer to Jeremy. "Why don't you want me with you? Anyone would think you don't *love* me anymore," she said, her voice whiny but also carrying an unmistakable edge to her words.

I shrank further into my chair, embarrassed on behalf of all womanhood for her display, and pulled my phone from my bag again. 8:23. Come on, Gemma and Susan. Where are you, and why on Earth didn't we just meet up in the corridor outside our rooms? I glanced towards the lift and debated going to their rooms to fetch them. Only the fear of my footsteps echoing on the floor and drawing attention my way stilled my steps.

Out of the corner of my eye, I noticed Jeremy pull the woman in for a hug and whisper something in her ear. From the look that crossed her face, I could tell she felt as though she'd won something. He pulled away and landed a kiss on her lips before motioning to the seated area and suggesting she take a seat while he checked in.

My eyes darted around the lounge area. Accompanied as she was by her entourage, the only place she would have to sit was in the cluster of chairs between the man whose eyes were now glued to his phone as though his life depended on it and me.

I shouldn't have worried about her bodyguards. They stayed outside the lounge area and watched all points of entry to the room as though expecting an attack.

As she passed, she glared down her nose at me, and then lifted her chin and turned away as if disgusted by what she saw. I straightened my dress and clasped tightly onto my hands, telling myself it would be petty to use a little magic to make her fall on her smug face. In contrast, she turned her attention to the man in the blue shirt and flashed him a smile. Much to my amusement, he refused to even acknowledge her presence and instead pulled his phone closer to his face.

When she flashed me with a second look that indicated I was no better than something she might stand on in the street, I decided I'd had enough of waiting and no longer cared if the clip-clop of my heels drew attention. Plus, if I was honest with myself, the need to make some slight calamity befall the woman was becoming far too much of a temptation.

My hand flew to the Melody Stone around my neck. The sacred seven was made naturally from Amethyst, Cacoxenite, Rutile, Goethite, Clear Quartz, Smoky Quartz, and Lepidocrocite. It enhanced my abilities to move objects. I'd crafted two pendants, one for me and one for Fleur, and insisted we wore them always. With it, we could move mountains. In theory. Not that I would need its power now. I just found it reassuring to know it was with me.

I could move the vase on the table without its help. I mean... a little nudge would see the flowers and water cascade over her...

No. I shook my head. Far better I left. I stood and walked back to the lift, keeping my head high and my gaze directly forward. Before I had the chance to reach the doors, they pinged open. Susan was mid-step out when I barrelled her back in.

"Eira," she barked when she almost stumbled into Gemma. "What *are* you doing?"

"Sorry," I said and slammed my finger into the close-door button. It was silly, I knew, but the last thing I wanted was to turn around now that I'd resolved to go to the lift. We could get off on another floor and walk around to the bar. "I'll explain later. There's a horrid woman in the lounge and I'd rather not have to look at her again."

Gemma puffed up and pushed past Susan. "What did she do?" she demanded, and I had to grab hold of her arm to stop her charging through the doors.

"Nothing particular," I said, inwardly smiling that Gemma seemed ready to fight for me.

She managed a quick glance out of the lift and then darted her head back inside before pressing the close-door button herself and selecting the next floor up. "Vanessa Brookes," was all she said as the doors finally closed and the lift rumbled back to life.

"Who?" I asked.

"Really?" Susan said at the same time.

"Hmm, hmm, in the lounge. Real as life, wearing a black dress that couldn't be shorter if it were a belt."

"That's the horrid woman I told you about. Do you know her?"

"Do we know her?" Susan asked, her face incredulous. "How do you not?"

"Vanessa Brookes. The reality TV star. Her face is always on one magazine cover or another. Come on, you're bound to have seen her before," Gemma added.

I shrugged. "Not my sort of thing. But it doesn't matter, anyway. Let's just get to the bar and enjoy our night. I'd much rather forget about ever laying eyes on Vanessa Brookes or whatever her name is and have fun just as we'd planned. She can go her merry way with Jeremy Dancer, and we can go ours."

"Jeremy Dancer," Gemma said and looked for all the world as though she might press the button to send the lift back down to the reception. "We missed everything."

"She was with Jeremy?" Susan asked. Her face looked a little sad, and a pang of guilt overtook me. I'd selfishly forced them both back into the lift because I'd been uncomfortable. So, what if I hadn't wanted to gawp at celebrities? Well… any more than I already had. That didn't mean I had the right to deprive my friends of the privilege.

"I'm sure we'll get the chance to see them together tomorrow at the competition," I said. "Jeremy is a judge, after all."

Susan flashed me a smile that didn't quite reach her eyes. "Of course. Let's get that drink," she said, and looped her arms between mine and Gemma's just as the elevator doors opened.

CHAPTER TWO

Ten minutes later, with our first drink downed, we decided to head to the Grill restaurant and grab some dinner. Cedar wood beams and stone walls gave the place a somewhat Canadian feel. Given the heat of the day, the open fires remained unlit, but I could imagine the warmth and comfort they gave off during the winter months. We were seated at a lovely table near the window that looked out over the stunning hotel grounds. Up high on the hillside, surrounded by fields and the golf course, and in turn trees, you could be forgiven for thinking you were miles away from civilisation and that the city of Newport was more than a stone's throw away. Happy chatter filled the air, along with the hustle and bustle of the servers as they took orders and brought drinks, along with plates filled with splendid meals arranged to catch the eye.

Although I was personally a gin drinker, I'd found myself drinking more and more vodka in Susan's presence, purely because it was her preference and that was usually what she had to hand. When I'd discovered the bar had a selection of not one or two but rather fifteen different gins, I decided to assert my own nature and resist Susan's offer of a raspberry vodka concoction. I couldn't make it through every gin on offer, not in one night, but I was determined to give it a go. I sipped at my orange marmalade gin, savoured its sweet citrus flavour that blended perfectly with the piney juniper, and surveyed the menu.

"The salmon sounds delicious," I said, fish always being a firm favourite of mine. I had been the same since I was small and had often suspected my bond to my cat, Niles, was the reason for it.

"Don't you dare go straight to the main course," Susan admonished. "We're doing this properly. Three courses at least."

Gemma laughed and patted her stomach. "It's a good job I'm starving," she said and shook her head. We both knew better than to argue with Susan. Even if we protested, she would probably order us three courses, anyway. It's just as well everything on the menu sounded delicious. My stomach rumbled and my mouth watered just thinking about all the food.

Our courses came, one after the other, and we enjoyed every bite of them. The buzz of the restaurant faded into the background as Gemma ran a running commentary on some of the food. Apparently, her sourdough bun was to die for and the spiced batter a dream. She hummed while eating them. I didn't think I'd ever seen anyone enjoy food quite the way she did. Susan laughed at her and asked if she should be making notes in order to update the menu for the café.

"That might not be a bad idea," Gemma said, and laughed along.

An hour and twenty minutes later, I sat back in my chair with a full belly and sipped at my sixth gin of the evening. This one, a delightful elderflower flavour. Normally, five gins in, I'd be more than a little tipsy, but with all the food I'd eaten — a beetroot and cherry tomato salad, followed by grilled salmon with baby potatoes, grilled vegetables, and a soy dressing, and then an indulgent maple-glazed waffle with peanut butter mousse, toffee sauce and banana ice-cream — I felt ready to go for another five.

"Where did you learn about all the crystals and oils?" Gemma asked as we sat at the table.

"My mother was into them when I was little. She taught me most of what I know, but I kept up my studies after she died." I brushed away Gemma and Susan's sympathies as soon as they offered them. "Although I miss her daily, it was a long, long time ago. That's one of the reasons I was so glad to find the cottage and shop and move to Caerleon after my divorce. It's where I'm from originally."

"Really?" Gemma asked, and I nodded. "What about you?" She continued, turning her attention to Susan. "Have you ever been married?"

Susan looked into the distance for a moment before shaking her head. "Marriage isn't for me. It could never satisfy me, settling down with just one person. There are far too many beautiful men and women in the world."

I shifted my cutlery and avoided looking anywhere but my plate for a few seconds. Susan had loved Tanya, that much had been clear. I sighed and wondered how different things could have been for her if they'd got together. It was tragic.

Given her feelings for Tanya, when we'd first met, I assumed Susan's romantic preference to be for women, but I'd soon learned that she enjoyed the company of both men and women in equal amounts. Although she protested, the romantic in me couldn't help but wish she would find someone to make her happy, one special person to spend the rest of her life with.

I sipped at my gin and wondered about the possibility of my finding the same thing. "How long have you and Lee been together?" I asked Gemma.

"Since we were nineteen," she answered. "He's my one and only love, and the best man I could ever hope to meet."

"Aww," Susan said and raised her glass. "Here's to true love."

"To true love," Gemma and I echoed with a smile.

"Actually, after we'd been dating for about a year, we found out that even though we went to different schools, we knew some of the same people and went to some of the same parties when we were as young as thirteen. Wouldn't it be funny if it turned out we all went to the same school? There's not many years between us. I don't suppose either of you went to Charles Williams, did you?"

Susan shook her head. "I went private," she said, and they both turned their attention to me.

"Home schooled," I answered.

"Oh, that's a shame. Still, I bet we played in the same parks and borrowed our books from the same library. It's funny how life turns out sometimes and what brings people together."

"I'll drink to that," Susan said, raising her glass, and we all laughed.

After a few more toasts, we left the table and returned to the bar. Within minutes, Susan was flirting with the bartender. She leaned on the bar, her blonde shoulder-length hair cloaking her face from view. I smiled, knowing that her face wasn't where the young man serving her was looking. With her low-cut neckline, his gaze rested elsewhere. The barman was twenty years her junior. He was exceptionally good-looking, with tanned skin and deep brown eyes that twinkled when he laughed at Susan's jokes. Many a glance was thrown his way by much younger women in the room than Susan, but perhaps in their youth, they lacked the confidence she possessed in speaking to him. Not that he was oblivious to their admiration. He knew how attractive he was and used it, no doubt, to gain generous tips amongst other amusements.

The thought brought my mind back to the encounter I'd witnessed in the reception. I'd judged Vanessa Brookes harshly. It wasn't like me to take an instant dislike to people, and I couldn't possibly know enough about her and Jeremy Dancer's relationship to reach any conclusions about the scene I witnessed.

"What gin are you on now?" Gemma called, her voice raised to be heard above the murmur of chatter and clink of glasses.

I lifted my glass and downed the remains of the London Dry. "The grapefruit one, I think," I answered.

Gemma opened her mouth to say something, but whatever it was, she cut off and pointed frantically behind me, her eyes wide.

I turned and focused my eyes across the barely lit room. Jeremy Dancer had arrived with the much younger Vanessa Brookes on his arm. They'd changed from their travelling clothes, and Vanessa now wore a red off-the-shoulder bodycon dress. Jeremy wore a jacket over a plain white T-shirt and khaki trousers. Their entourage had reduced to just four men, each puffing their chests and trying to look tough and menacing. Given my slightly inebriated state, I bit back a laugh at their efforts, which were somewhat diminished by the fact they were all wearing dark glasses. Given the time of day and the subdued lighting in the bar, I doubted they could see more than two feet in front of their faces.

The entrance of the famous pair caused quite a stir, and even Susan's flirtatious bartender shifted his attention from her to the newcomers. From the increased chatter around me, it appeared I was the only person in existence who hadn't heard of Vanessa prior to today. Of the two, you'd think she was the more famous.

Susan finally realised her companion's focus was now elsewhere and turned to look at what all the fuss was about. Her face flickered with some unknown emotion for a moment before she recovered her composure, bade a good evening to the handsome young man, and returned to stand by me with her back to the celebrity couple.

"Where were we?" she asked, clapping her hands together as though we were in the middle of some nefarious plan and she needed us to refocus.

Gemma arrived, carrying three glasses in a triangle between her fingers. "Gin for you." She nodded at me and the glass on the left where a sprig of rosemary garnished the pink icy liquid. "Vodka and cranberry for you." A nod to the right and the red vodka garnished with mint. "And a white wine and Creme de Mure for me," she added, licking her lips, and taking a sip from her blackberry adorned wine glass after we'd relieved her of our drinks.

"Let's find a quiet corner away from all the fuss," Susan said after downing her drink and calling to the bartender for another.

We inched towards the far side of the room and found

ourselves an empty table.

"I'm half tempted to go over and introduce myself to Jeremy," Gemma said as soon as she sat. "Do you think that's a bad idea?"

"Why would it be a bad idea?" Susan asked, although I thought Gemma might have a point.

"We wouldn't want to be seen cosying up to one of the judges on the eve of the baking competition," I suggested.

Susan took a slow sip of her glass. "You might be right. We wouldn't want people to think him biased in your favour, especially after Jeremy did us a huge favour and allowed your late entry."

CHAPTER THREE

"What?" Gemma and I both said at the same time. Not once had Susan mentioned knowing Jeremy Dancer.

Susan winced and glanced at Gemma as if she realised that she'd blurted something out she hadn't meant to. Copious amounts of alcohol will do that for you. She sighed and placed her glass firmly on the wooden tabletop before reaching over and taking hold of Gemma's hand. "I told you, I had an old friend who might be able to see if there was time to enter you," she said.

"Yes, but I didn't realise that old friend was Jeremy Dancer." Gemma eyed her suspiciously and a flash of worry crossed her face. "This is terrible. You used your influence to get me a spot. I knew I wasn't good enough to enter any competitions."

"Don't be ridiculous," Susan said. "You're here on the merits of your cooking and those alone. I merely sent a few of your samples to Jeremy, and he confirmed what I've known all along. You are an absolute treasure of a baker."

Gemma blushed and took a sip from her wineglass. The doubt

on her face was plain to see. Ever since Susan had persuaded her to sign up, she'd wavered between feeling ecstatic and like she was about to make a fool of herself. It didn't matter that she ran a very successful café, which garnered rave reviews for the quality of its food and the welcoming of its staff. This new development, the night before the competition, not to mention the paranoia-inducing effects alcohol can sometimes bring forth, was the last thing she needed.

Seeing her new friend's agony, Susan downed her drink once again and stood. "Come on," she said. "We're going to speak to Jeremy. If I can't convince you how amazing you are, maybe he will."

When Gemma seemed reluctant to move, Susan grabbed her hand and motioned for me to grab the other. I wasn't particularly looking forward to having any form of interaction with Vanessa again, but if speaking to Jeremy was what Gemma needed, then that's what we were going to do. Besides, maybe it was only right that I should give the young reality TV star a chance.

"Jeremy, darling," Susan said as soon as we were within earshot. She released Gemma's arm and flung hers wide. Jeremy glanced up and instantly became alert. His eyes shone, and a wide smile split his face as he stepped forward. Much to my relief, Vanessa had moved away and was deep in conversation on the other side of the room with one of their security.

"Susan, I am glad to see you."

They held each other in a warm embrace for a few seconds before Susan pulled back and kissed Jeremy on both cheeks.

"It's been far too long," she said.

"That it has." He stepped back and looked at her. "You look amazing," he said and twirled her around.

Susan giggled like a love-struck schoolgirl. "You've barely aged a day."

Jeremy beamed down at her. "I feel like I've aged a million," he said, but Susan batted his words away as nonsense.

Gemma linked her arm in mine and whispered something about making ourselves scarce. At that moment, I had to agree, but when we turned to leave, Susan pulled us right back.

"I would like you to meet two dear friends of mine," she said. "Eira, Gemma, I have the pleasure of introducing Jeremy Dancer, chef, judge, and a delightful rogue. The scoundrel stole my heart many years ago and never gave it back."

Jeremy laughed and looked at Susan with undisguised affection. "Actually, ladies, I think you'll find that it was the other way around."

Susan sucked in a deep breath and seemed to take a moment to compose herself. A group of women in their fifties stepped between her and Jeremy, holding their phones high and asking for a picture.

He obliged, but excused himself immediately after, and stepped between them to pull Susan back to the forefront.

"As popular as ever," she said and smiled.

Jeremy shrugged. He paused as though thinking of something, his eyes distant. "Remember this," he said after a moment and delved into his pocket and pulled out an old pocket watch.

Susan gasped and clutched her hand over the top of his, engulfing the watch. "After all this time, you still have it," she said, her eyes glazing over.

"It was the last thing you gave me. Of course, I still have it." Jeremy smiled at her.

I shifted my feet, wondering if *now* might be the best time for me and Gemma to leave. Susan and Jeremy had obviously been in a close relationship at some point, and if the way they looked at each other was anything to go by, feelings remained.

"Believe me when I say that the situation would have to be pretty dire for me to part with it," Jeremy continued.

Susan sighed and took a deep breath before turning to me and Gemma as if suddenly remembering we were there. "Now," she said, pulling Gemma closer. "I'm not sure if we're breaking any rules in talking to you before the competition, but I wanted to make sure you met the fabulous baker I discovered."

Jeremy cleared his throat, pocketed the watch, and stilled

whatever emotions raced inside him before reaching out to shake Gemma's hand. "When Susan said how good you were, I have to confess to being a little doubtful, but then she sent me a selection of your patisseries and my goodness," he punctuated his words by kissing his fingers and flicking them in the air. "I don't know where you've been hiding, but I cannot wait to taste your creations tomorrow." The entire time, he kept one arm wrapped around Susan.

Gemma blushed some more, and unlike her normal self, came over all bashful and at a loss for words. No doubt, her head was swimming with the dizzying effects of alcohol. I'd started to feel a little unsteady on my feet and at times the ground seemed to wobble and the crowd sway. We needed to call it a night and be thankful that Gemma didn't have to check in for the competition until one in the afternoon.

"And by the process of elimination, you must be Eira," Jeremy said, and turned his winning smile on me. "It's a pleasure to meet you. I saw you earlier in reception, if I'm not mistaken," he added. It was my turn to blush. I had hoped he'd forgotten my staring at him like some star-struck teenager. "It's great to see Susan so happy and in the company of good friends," he added.

I was about to say how I thought Susan's happiness stemmed more from seeing him when, once again, a shrill voice cut through the air, calling out to Jeremy.

We all turned to the sound and saw Vanessa striding towards him. She placed her hand possessively on his shoulder and dragged him away from Susan. Her face twisted in a scowl, and she leaned in to whisper something in his ear, then pulled back and flicked her pink hair dramatically over her shoulder. "Let's go back to the suite and open my bottle of Chateau Montelena," she said loud enough to be heard by everyone while snaking her arms around his waist. "I'm bored with all these *Welsh* people."

Jeremy's smile faltered for a second. "Vanessa, it's unbecoming to be rude to our host nation or the people who have welcomed us so warmly," he said in slight admonishment.

Vanessa glanced around, as if pretending to notice our

presence for the first time. Once again, she looked down her nose at me and added the others to her obvious disdain. And once again, I had an almost irresistible urge to make something unpleasant befall her. I cleared my throat and shook the thought from my head. Yes. It was most definitely time to call it a night. With my inhibitions lowered, who knew what I might do?

I turned my attention back to Jeremy. "It was a pleasure to meet *you*," I said, purposely excluding Vanessa from the comment, and making it clear that we were about to take our leave.

He cleared his throat. "You too," he said. "All of you. Susan, we'll have to catch up later," he added, and much to Vanessa's chagrin, pulled out of little Miss High-and-Mighty's arms and pulled Susan in for a quick peck goodbye. "It really is good to see you," he said.

Susan gave him a weak smile, and I wondered what had happened between them in the past and whether she would ever decide to tell me. Losing Tanya had been hard for her. I so hoped her reunion with Jeremy would not drag her back down into another pit of despair.

Both my body and heart felt heavy when the three of us linked arms and moved away from Jeremy. I couldn't understand what he saw in Vanessa Brooke. As a couple, they somehow didn't seem to fit, and not because of the age difference. He was warm and friendly; she was cold and showed little respect for anyone. Still, it was their choice to be together.

"So, which was it?" Gemma asked as soon as we were out of the bar and walking along the hotel corridor. "Did he steal your heart, or did you steal his?"

Susan laughed. "It was a very, very long time ago," she said. "Far too long to remember all the details."

"Not too long ago for him to look at you like you were the love of his life," Gemma said and hiccupped.

I glanced at Susan to see her reaction. Her eyes stared blankly ahead as if she was lost in thought. She must have sensed me looking as she gave me a forlorn smile, which I returned.

"Come on," she said after a moment. "We'd better get to bed."

A WORD TO THE WITCH

CHAPTER FOUR

I woke the next morning feeling somewhat worse for wear. I opened my eyes and squinted.

"Bright light, bright light." I cursed, wincing at the sound of my own voice. My head pounded with dizzying waves of pain that matched the nausea in my stomach. I felt like hell, and my mouth felt as though something furry had crawled inside and died. I slunk back under the duvet and wished for darkness to claim me, but knowing my deep need to snuggle under the covers and sleep the day away to be an impossibility, I grumbled, sat up, and reached for the water on the bedside table.

After my useless attempt at alleviating my thirst, I dragged myself from the bed and went straight to the tea-making facilities to boil some water. A cup of magically infused ginseng tea wouldn't cure all my hangover symptoms, but it would make the day bearable, and with any luck, I'd be able to grab a few hours' rest after the competition before we had another evening of entertainment. I could only thank my good fortune that I'd had the foresight to pack some. My magic might not work to its full power for me, but at least I could pass some onto Gemma and Susan and make them feel like fully functioning humans again.

After drinking the tea and making a mental note to teach Fleur the spell involved in its creation as soon as humanly possible, I brushed my teeth thoroughly, showered, and then dressed in a light summer skirt and a sleeveless white blouse that tied at the waist. My hair I left free in all its wild, untamed glory. After adding a little foundation to my face to hide the dark circles that rimmed my eyes, I decided to brave the outside world.

The hallway was even brighter than my room, but the tea had worked a minor miracle, and I no longer felt like a gremlin who needed to stay away from bright lights for fear of boiling over into a pile of slime.

"Good morning," I said to Susan as soon as she opened her door in her dressing gown. Her blonde hair, which normally brushed her shoulders in soft waves, looked as if she'd spent the night back-combing it into a tangled mess. Mascara surrounded her eyes, giving her a panda bear look.

"What time is it?" she asked and rubbed her hand over the back of her neck.

"Almost eleven," I answered, and Susan groaned. "I wondered if it might be an idea to grab some food before we head to the competition."

Susan looked as though she was about to throw up at the mere suggestion. "I don't think I can," she said and covered her mouth.

I glanced down the corridor towards Gemma's room and hoped she was in better shape than Susan. "Shower and get dressed. I'll be back for you at 12:30," I said while reaching into my bag for some of my ginseng tea. I grabbed Susan's hand and placed the tea firmly in her palm. "Promise me you'll make this up and drink it," I added.

"Will it make me feel less like death on legs?" she asked.

"Most definitely."

Susan braved a smile. "Then you can bet I'll drink it. I have enough experience with your concoctions to know how well they work." Her eyes flicked along the corridor and returned to my face. Her shoulders slumped, and she tried to hand the tea back. "You'd better give this to Gemma," she said. "She's the one that needs to be on her best game today."

I pressed it back into her hand. "I have enough for everyone," I said, smiling.

"Oh, thank *bleep* for that," she said and sagged in relief, although bleep wasn't the exact word she used. She clutched the tea tight to her chest and confirmed she'd be all ready for the afternoon when I came back to collect her.

Two minutes later, I knocked on Gemma's door. Much to my surprise, she was wide awake and as bright as a daisy. She beamed at me and invited me in.

"You look to be faring better than me and Susan this morning," I said and noted the breakfast tray on the small table.

"I'm not at all surprised," Gemma said. "Not with the way the two of you were knocking back vodka and gin. Besides, I've never been much of a one for getting hangovers."

I'd never thought of myself as a big drinker, but thinking back to the night before, it was easy to see how much I'd consumed compared to Gemma. I must have gone through three drinks to every one of hers, and on top of that, my gin was at least 40 proof. Susan must have had more again.

"Well, not that you need it," I reached into my bag and produced the tea, "but this will give you a boost of energy and a clear head for this afternoon. I was going to see if you wanted to grab some food..." I glanced at her empty plate.

"Ah, yes. I tried to knock on your doors earlier to see if either of you were awake, but when no one answered—"

I raised my hand to stop her needless explanation. I vaguely recalled a knocking from my dream, but had been too deep in slumber to respond. After Gemma confirmed she was going to spend the next hour or so going through her notes and making sure she was mentally prepared for the competition, I excused myself and told her I'd be back to meet up with her and Susan later.

As I walked along the corridor, I debated going back to my

room and ordering breakfast in the way Gemma had, but decided against the idea. The day was fresh and bright, and a walk in the open air would do me wonders. If I was lucky, I could grab an outside table and enjoy some food on the terrace.

I stepped from the elevator and into the lobby feeling better for making the decision, and had to admit, after an early lunch of a wild mushroom, sun-blushed tomato, and spinach filo parcel, complete with basil polenta and several large glasses of water, I felt almost myself again.

I sat at my table on the terrace as my plates were cleared and glanced inside at the restaurant. I wasn't the only person eating alone, but there weren't many of us.

"Is there anything else I can get you, Ma'am?" the waitress asked, and I opted for a glass of fresh orange juice.

As I waited for her to return, I tuned out the chatter of other guests and focused on the electronic whir of the golf carts as they traversed the well-tended green. I loved the smell of freshly mown grass and the soft kiss of the breeze as the sun warmed my skin. I could have stayed there all day, but as soon as I'd finished my juice, I glanced at my phone, and finding some time to spare, I took a quick walk around the grounds and checked in with Fleur to make sure everything was okay.

"Everything's fine," she said.

"Abby's behaving?"

"We ran through some exercises this morning. I closed up shop a little while ago and now we're in the workshop going through the properties of various oils."

"That's good." If Abby was to be as much help to Fleur as Niles was to me, she'd need to discover what worked best for our various spells. I continued along the meandering path. I'd walked beyond the car park and to the side of the golf course and found a grassy area surrounded by mature trees. Their leaves saved my skin from the burning sun. "Ask her what's a good headache buster?" I asked.

Fleur laughed. "Feeling a bit worse for wear, are we?"

"Not anymore, but you should have seen me an hour ago."

Fleur laughed again, but moments later her muffled voice carried along the line. "Abby has selected both lavender and peppermint," she said as soon as she returned. "You are such a clever girl," she added in a baby voice, and I smiled, knowing she was talking to the cat.

"You should join us for dinner this evening. Unless you have other plans. Abby needs to get used to being left alone. Niles can watch her for a few hours," I added.

"It would be nice to get out," she agreed.

"That's settled then. I'll speak to you later."

After the call, I sucked in a deep breath of fresh air and went back inside, ready to meet with Susan and Gemma, but as soon as I entered the reception, I froze in my tracks. Detective Inspector Kate McIntyre stood talking to the hotel manager at the front desk. From the serious look on her face, I knew she was here on business.

Before I could decide whether or not to acknowledge her presence, she spotted me.

"Eira," she called and waved me down before turning to the hotel manager and excusing herself from their conversation.

As usual, she'd tied her hair back in a ponytail, and she looked all business in her light grey suit. She strode purposefully towards me with a scowl on her face. I tried not to wince as her every step echoed on the tiled floor.

"Eira," she said again in a tone that suggested her being there was somehow my fault.

"Kate," I responded with wide-eyed innocence. "I wasn't expecting to see you here."

I'd only seen Kate on a handful of occasions since we'd solved Tanya's case. She was convinced I knew something about a panther that was spotted rushing through the common on the night I'd been taken hostage by the murderer. She was right. Tanya's sister had whacked me over the head with a frying pan and tied me to a chair. Niles shifted and came to my rescue.

Sometimes I wondered if Kate was too clever for her own good. There was no chance I'd ever admit to what really happened, but she knew I was hiding something, and that had made our interactions a little less friendly than I would have liked at times.

Kate tilted her head to the side in her peculiar dog-like manner and huffed out a breath. "And yet somehow I'm not surprised to see you," she said. "Do you want to tell me why that is?"

I rolled my eyes and shrugged. "I can't begin to guess why you think one thing or another, but if this is your way of asking me why I'm here, I'm here for the baking competition that starts this afternoon. A friend of mine has entered."

Kate stared at me for a while without responding. If anything, my words had caused her to look at me with even more distrust. "You know, I was wrong to say you were no Miss Marple," she said, referencing her warning to me not to investigate Tanya's murder. "It would seem that crime follows wherever you go."

I bristled at her statement. Kate knew full well that my ex-husband Chris was a con artist serving time. She also knew that it was my evidence that put him there. And how in the world could she hold me responsible for discovering Tanya's body? Especially as she knew I'd been set up to do just that.

I was about to give her a piece of my mind when my mouth froze on opening. For Kate to be here, something had to have happened, and I'd bet money on it not being something good. My anger faded as quickly as it had arrived, and a tightness I hadn't realised I was holding left my brow. "What happened?" I asked.

Instead of answering my question, Kate crooked her finger and motioned for me to follow.

Several minutes later, we stepped out of the elevator on the top floor of the hotel and arrived outside a guarded suite. The police officer on the door slid a plastic card into the lock and stepped aside.

A delicious citrus scent wafted on the air as soon as we entered. I almost gasped. I'd thought my room fancy with its deluxe king-size bed and a sitting area to the side complete with a sofa and two armchairs, but it had nothing on the room I now entered. It was easily three times the size of my room, with no bed in sight. Two red and golden armchairs faced one side of a central coffee table, with a surface big enough to comfortably lay out a meal for four. A large glass vase decorated its centre, overflowing with white oriental lilies. Next to this stood an open bottle of red wine and a single unused glass. A pair of cushioned four-seater sofas faced the table from the left and right, and the end tables to either side of these gave home to four emerald-green table lamps with pure white, pleated shades. Most striking of all were the three sets of windows that lined the back wall. Each set was bigger than the entire front of my shop and framed with red velvet curtains.

I swallowed and nodded to the police officers standing by a door to the right side of the room, doing my best not to fidget and look nervous. Kate motioned for them to open the door. I followed her inside.

CHAPTER FIVE

Jeremy Dancer was lying on the bed in the same T-shirt and trousers he'd worn the night before. His jacket rested on the back of a chair next to the window. I huffed out a breath and surveyed his pale face. It was angled towards another side door, his eyes wide open and staring.

My only thought as I stared at his lifeless body was, poor Susan. She'd already lost someone close to her, and now she'd lost another dear friend.

Not wanting to dwell on the body, I glanced around the bedroom. It was as opulent as the lounge, but a faint musty smell hung in the air.

Kate watched me; her eyebrows drawn together.

I rested my hand on my stomach and closed my eyes. Now would not be a good time for Jeremy's ghost to appear. As much as I wanted to know what had happened to him, I couldn't risk talking to him in front of Kate. It had been bad enough when I'd had to talk to Tanya's spirit, but at least Kate wasn't as suspicious of me then as she was now. She'd be watching for any sign of the unusual, and who knows how I might react. It's not as though I dealt with the dead every day. I'd caught the odd fleeting glimpse of spirits around the village since Tanya, but none had been recently deceased, and none had felt a pressing need to communicate with me. As long as they were content to keep their own business, so too was I.

I sighed and turned to Kate. She may have had vague suspicions regarding my keeping secrets from her, but there was no way she could tie Jeremy's death to anything I'd done.

"Why did you bring me here?" I asked, my voice strained.

Kate's eyes brimmed with questions. "Did you know the victim?" she asked.

"I knew of him, but I think almost everyone does. I did speak with him for a few minutes last night."

Kate raised an eyebrow at my last statement and motioned one of the officers over to take notes. I glanced at his face and realised we'd met before over a different body. His name was Officer Johnson, if I remembered correctly. He smiled at me and pulled his pen and pad from his pocket.

"When did you see him?" Kate asked.

"We were in the Grill bar. We left straight after and went to sleep in our rooms." I glanced at the officer as he jotted down what I said. "You have to understand that I was a little drunk at the time, so knowing exactly when that was is hard to pin down — We use key cards to enter the rooms, there must be some sort of log — He was still there when we left." I looked over Jeremy's body and wondered what could have befallen him. He was charming and full of life when we'd seen him in the bar. I couldn't see any obvious wounds or signs of a struggle, but Kate's presence told me that she thought something was amiss. "What about the woman he was with? Vanessa Brookes. She's some sort of reality TV star. Maybe she'd be able to give you an idea of when they left. She mentioned being bored and asked to return to the room."

Kate nodded. "I had the opportunity to speak with Ms Brookes downstairs." Despite myself, I couldn't help the small sliver of satisfaction at the tone of Kate's voice when she mentioned Vanessa. It would seem she'd taken as much of a dislike to her as I had. "By her account, Mr Dancer was pestered by, and I quote 'three inebriated middle-aged *bleeps*' last night, and she had to rescue him from their unwanted advances. He'd decided to go for a walk after that. Ms Brookes was exhausted and not wanting to be disturbed when he returned, opted to sleep in one of the other bedrooms."

I scoffed at that and shook my head. That would be her version of events, and just as she'd lied about our interaction with Jeremy, I had no doubt in my mind that she was also lying about *choosing* to sleep in another room.

"What about their security?" I asked. "When I saw the pair arrive yesterday evening, they had a large group of men with them, bodyguards of sorts. Four accompanied them to the bar last night."

Kate eyeballed me. "Then last night wasn't the only time you met with Mr Dancer."

I huffed out a breath and rubbed my head. "Stop looking for secrets where there aren't any," I snapped, no longer caring to keep my tone civil. "I was in the reception lounge waiting for my friends before heading out to dinner when Mr Dancer arrived. I did not speak to him at that time, but I did witness an uncomfortable exchange between him and Ms Brookes." Kate nodded for me to continue. "She wasn't pleased with being here. He said that she'd been free to stay at home. It was clearly something they'd argued about previously, and she'd turned into a manipulative bawler to get her own way. You can ask their security and the reception staff about that too. I wasn't the only one subjected to her performance."

Before I had the chance to say anything else, a commotion sounded from the lounge area. Kate sighed and headed out of the bedroom. I gave Jeremy's body one final glance. Noting his unseeing gaze directed towards the ensuite, I followed it and saw a second empty wine glass resting on the counter next to the sink. I was half tempted to take a closer look, but instead followed Kate.

As if drawn by the mention of her name, Vanessa Brookes stood in the doorway screaming and demanding entry. One of her bodyguards stood behind her. With a stamp of her foot, she declared that she needed her bag, and that she was not happy they were keeping her away from her possessions.

Far from a grieving girlfriend, she behaved more like an entitled harpy, and when she saw me, her screeching increased.

"She did it," she bellowed and waved her phone-filled hand in my direction. "Her and her friends. They were all over my poor Jeremy last night."

Kate rubbed at her eyes before plastering a fake smile on her face and raising her hand. "If you would kindly stop shouting, we can discuss the allegations you are levelling at Ms Snow and her friends."

Vanessa scowled at me, but stopped her bleating, and attempted to push further into the room. After a nod from Kate to the officer guarding the door, he stepped aside and let her and only her enter. When her escort complained, Vanessa told him she'd be fine and not to make a fuss. I scoffed at that. If anyone was making a fuss, it was her.

"Take a seat," Kate said and motioned Vanessa to one of the sofas. "Eira, you too."

Vanessa's face beamed at this comment. She sat, pulled her dress down slightly, and started tapping away on her phone.

I perched on the edge of the sofa and rested my hand on its plush cushion.

Kate walked over and took the phone from Vanessa's hand.

"Ugh, rude," Vanessa said and tried to snatch it back.

Kate handed it to her. "You may consider my actions rude, but what you are about to post would be deemed libel. I suggest you delete anything you have to say regarding Ms Snow."

My mouth dropped open as I realised with shock that Vanessa must have been about to declare me a murderer on whatever social media platform she favoured. How dare she. I almost wished Kate hadn't stopped her. I'd have loved to wipe the smirk from her face after seeing her in court.

"Now," said Kate calmly, before taking a seat next to me. "Whilst the death of Mr Dancer is undoubtedly tragic, we are yet to confirm the cause of death. I would be very much interested to know why you believe he was murdered?"

This sparked my curiosity. I didn't want to be involved, but as I was feeling more than a little indignant about being accused, that ship had already sailed.

Vanessa glared at me again. I resisted rolling my eyes. I had honestly never met another single person in my life who annoyed me in the same way she did. Not even the woman who took delight in confirming her affair with my now ex-husband.

"People don't just die," Vanessa said and pursed her lips.

"Actually, they do."

I gave Kate a sideways glance. She was a good detective, stubborn, and pig-headed, but she worked hard and had a good heart under her sometimes cold exterior. It was clear from her tone and the way she questioned me that she believed Jeremy Dancer had been murdered, so what was she up to?

Vanessa crossed her arms and flung herself back in the chair with a dramatic swoosh of her pink hair. "He'd been distant," she said and crossed her arms. "Argumentative. Something was wrong."

For the first time, I saw a flash of humanity and caring in Vanessa's face, and had to remind myself that I knew nothing about her. I cursed myself for being so judgemental and vowed to do better in the future.

"I understand things may have been difficult recently," Kate said, "but what makes you think it was anything other than a simple bump in the course of your relationship? Mr Dancer was a good deal older than you. Maybe, he simply wanted different things."

"Age has nothing to do with love," Vanessa said, and started crying. "Something was wrong," she repeated. "And it had to do with coming here. That's why he didn't want me with him. That's why I know it was her and her friends," she said and pointed at me again. "I was with him the entire time, and they were the only people he spoke with."

"Apart from when he went on his walk," I interjected.

"What?"

I glanced at Kate and back at Vanessa. "You told the police that you slept in another room to avoid being disturbed when Mr Dancer came back from his walk. You couldn't have been with him then, or when he returned. How could you know who he did or didn't meet with?"

At this, Vanessa's bawling intensified. I shared a look with Kate, and she shrugged. Neither of us was used to a grown adult crying in the unrestrained manner of a two-year-old. I guessed we'd just have to ride it out. Thankfully, we didn't have to sit and wait for her to compose herself for long. Her phone rang in her hand, and as quickly as they started, her tears stopped.

"Daddy," she said and leapt to her feet. "You're here. Thank goodness. It's all so horrible. I'm in the suite… Yes, Daddy. I will…" She paced the room and scowled at Officer Johnson when he blocked the doorway leading to Jeremy. "No. I can't," she continued. "The police are questioning me… Okay… okay, Daddy. I will." Vanessa clutched the phone to her chest and turned to Kate. "Daddy said that I am not to talk to you anymore without my lawyer present. So, if you don't mind, I'd like to collect my things and leave."

Kate stood. "Your things need to be catalogued as part of the crime scene. We'd also like you to compose a list of the possessions Mr Dancer brought with him. It's important to know if anything's missing. I would also appreciate your cooperation in staying at the hotel. I'm sure they can arrange another room for you to use."

Vanessa looked indignant and pursed her lips. "As I've already offered to participate as a judge in the competition in Jeremy's absence, I was going to stay anyway," she said and flounced from the room and away with her waiting escort.

I flopped back in the seat and shook my head in disbelief. Jeremy's body wasn't even cold, and his girlfriend was stepping in to fill his role as judge. So much for a grieving period.

"The competition's still on?" I queried and glanced around the room, looking for a clock.

"Apparently. The management said they are shifting it to later in the day, but given the money they make with it going ahead, they weren't willing to cancel it altogether."

"Can't you make them?" I asked, but carried on before Kate could answer. "Sorry. I guess if you could, you would." I stood, deciding it was time I should leave. Susan and Gemma may have been told about the time delay, but it was doubtful they knew why. I'd rather Susan heard about Jeremy's death from me before she did anyone else. "Why do *you* think he was murdered?" I asked, turning to Kate.

"Did you notice the smell in the bedroom?"

"The musty one?"

"I've smelt it before in a case of hemlock poisoning." She looked at me pointedly. "Don't you keep hemlock in your store?"

I bristled but sat back down, finally understanding why Kate had entertained the possibility I might be involved. "I have hemlock *essential oil* in the store," I confirmed. "But it's a completely different substance to the poisonous one. The essential oil is distilled from a tree. It belongs to an entirely different genus and species. If I remember correctly, the toxin comes from a member of the parsley family, but the essential oil comes from the conifer tree."

"I did wonder," Kate said before asking Officer Johnson to make a note of what I'd said.

"Does this mean I'm no longer under suspicion?" I asked.

Kate laughed. "Until you start telling me the whole truth, you'll always be under suspicion," she said. I could tell she'd warmed to me as her eyes twinkled a little. I shifted, a little uneasy, knowing that she viewed me as a puzzle to solve, but at least it was better than being considered a murderer. "But I've no reason to believe you have anything to do with this case, if that's what you're asking," she continued.

I stood again and walked towards the door.

"But just in case, maybe you should stick around the hotel for a while, too."

I puffed myself up in much the same way Vanessa had. "I fully intended on staying for the baking competition anyway," I said, then turned with a swish of my skirt and stormed out the door, wondering if Gemma would still want to enter.

I froze two seconds later. "Oh, *bleep*!" I said and resisted stamping my foot — I didn't want to emulate all of Vanessa's bad habits — before turning back. Ms Brookes may be able to get away with her dramatic exit, but I couldn't, not with the thought that suddenly struck my mind.

"Jeremy Dancer was an accomplished chef," I said when Kate raised her eyebrow at my return. "His job entailed recognising and tasting food. Something would have to have a pretty strong flavour to hide it... or it would need to be something you might consume very quickly without giving yourself the chance to taste it." I pointed at the bottle of wine on the table. "I'm not sure what Chateau Montelena tastes like, but I can tell you that I've downed a glass or two of wine in my time without waiting to register its flavour."

I didn't wait for Kate's response before turning on my heels and leaving. Maybe I could pull off a dramatic exit after all.

CHAPTER SIX

"Fleur," I said as soon as she answered the phone. "I need your help."

"What's up?" she asked.

I smiled at the elderly couple dragging a suitcase along the corridor to their room and waited until they were out of earshot before answering. "There's been a murder."

"What? Really?"

I loved Fleur to pieces, but a small part of me wondered if I should be worried about the excitement she displayed every time something dastardly happened.

"Yes, really."

"Oh, wait. Susan and Gemma are both okay... aren't they?" she asked, her voice dropping.

I smiled, my faith in her restored. "They're both fine. But I'm not looking forward to telling Susan what's happened. The victim was a friend of hers."

"Not another one."

"My thoughts exactly." At this rate, the poor woman wouldn't have any friends left. I shuddered at the thought and tried not to dwell on what that meant for me. I had no more right to think crime followed Susan around than Kate did to think it followed me.

"Do you need me to come there?" Fleur asked.

Despite knowing how eager she'd be to be involved in all the action, I had to decline her offer, for now. "Not straight away. But can we meet a bit earlier than planned? I need you to look into hemlock... and before you ask, not the essential oil we use, the poisonous plant."

"Sure. I didn't know they were any different," she said, and I could hear the shrug in her voice. "What do you need to know?"

I ran off a list of everything I could think of, including how long it took to act, how much someone needed to ingest for it to be lethal, and what it looked like. "Find out as much as you can and meet me at the competition. It's been delayed until four." Niles would be fine taking care of Abby for a few hours more than originally planned.

"Okay, I'll see you... Wait, there's a picture of the hotel on the news." Fleur went quiet for a second, and I heard the volume on the TV increase in the background. "Jeremy Dancer's dead." She gasped and then almost screamed down the phone, "Was Jeremy Dancer murdered?"

I winced and glanced around to make sure no one was close enough to hear her shrieks. "Just keep that to yourself, for now. I'm not sure Kate is releasing that information to the wider public until it's confirmed."

"Oh, wow. Okay. I'll find out what I can and meet you later." Despite her words, I heard the uncharacteristic note of hesitation in her voice. "There's going to be press everywhere," she said when I asked her what was wrong. "Do you really want to get involved in a case that has that level of exposure?"

I hadn't thought about that. My previous involvement in a murder investigation had led to Kate suspecting me, even if she didn't know what she suspected me of. This case had the potential for a whole new level of scrutiny. Fleur was right to be wary. For both our sakes.

I ended the call as soon as I reached Susan's door with a promise that we'd discuss things when Fleur arrived, although a part of me had already decided we couldn't get involved. It was one thing to peddle my spell-infused oils with the goal of helping people, but the fewer people who knew I was actually a 'real' witch, as Fleur liked to call me, the better. Burning, drowning, and hanging of witches might be a thing of the past, but that didn't mean people wouldn't find a way to make life difficult.

After knocking for a few minutes, I concluded that Susan couldn't be in her room and edged along the corridor to Gemma's. She answered after the first two knocks.

"I was wondering where you were," she said as soon as I entered the room. "Did you hear? They've moved the start of the competition to four. We're doing the first bake today, and the remaining bake's been rescheduled for tomorrow morning."

I mumbled noncommittally and glanced around the room. "Have you seen Susan?" I asked, not seeing her and not hearing any sounds from the bathroom.

"She popped down to reception. Someone left a package for her. She shouldn't be long." I slumped in one of the armchairs and rubbed my head. Gemma sat opposite me. "Are you still feeling the effects of last night?" she asked with a slight smile at the edge of her lips.

I sighed and wished I was. A hangover would be far easier to deal with. Despite my condition on waking, the food, fresh air, and recent events had washed away all traces of my hangover, as well as my memory of it. "Jeremy Dancer's dead," I said, deciding it was better to tell Gemma. She'd have the chance to get over any shock before I told Susan.

Her hand flew to her mouth. "Oh, my God," she said. "That's why they've rescheduled. He… he seemed so fit and healthy when we spoke to him. I mean, he was in great shape. But I guess you never know… Oh, my God," she said again. "He didn't kill—"

"It's not a suicide."

"Thank goodness for that small blessing. I'm not sure how Susan would take such dreadful news. It's bad enough that he's passed."

This made me sink my head further into my hands. I huffed out a deep breath and looked through my splayed fingers at Gemma. Her enviable, straight brown hair was tied back in the neat bun she favoured when cooking, and she'd dressed in a sensible outfit of trousers, white shirt, and flat shoes. Her revision cards lay in a stack to the side of the chair. I didn't know why she'd felt it necessary to revise for anything. She could cook, at times, without the need to weigh ingredients, and her bakes always turned out perfect. Susan hadn't exaggerated when she'd said how brilliant Gemma was. But I knew how worried she'd been about her technical knowledge. She'd mentioned watching a TV baking competition once, and the judges had asked all sorts of questions relating to different pastries and bake styles. Gemma was a natural cook and hadn't felt the need to learn all the fancy names.

"Jeremy didn't kill himself," I said, echoing my previous statement. "But if the Detective Inspector is right, he was very likely murdered."

I didn't have the chance to gauge Gemma's reaction to the news because the room door burst open and Susan barged through. She sagged against the door as soon as it shut while holding a package in her hands, and closed her eyes.

Gemma and I were up and beside her side in an instant. "I'm so sorry, Susan," Gemma said and pulled her in for a big hug. Neither of us needed to ask if she'd heard about Jeremy.

I cursed not going to the reception to fetch her. I should have realised as soon as Fleur said about Jeremy's death being on the news that it would soon be all around the hotel. I reached out and placed my hand on Susan's. She pulled back and looked at me. For the first time, I noticed the fingers gripping the package in her hand were white.

"Let's get you into a chair with a nice cup of tea," I said, pulling her to her feet.

When I tried to take the package, Susan realised how tightly she'd been gripping it. Her hands opened in a startled pop and she flexed her fingers. Gemma and I helped her to the chair, where she sat looking into the room with an unseeing gaze, seemingly numb. I placed the unopened package to the side next to Gemma's cards. Whatever was inside could wait.

I rummaged in my bag for something to help. I hadn't thought to bring any supplies, but the refreshing ginseng tea would help clear her thoughts. Gemma tried to comfort Susan while I made the tea.

Susan's hand shook as she took the cup from me. "I'm so sorry," was all I could think to say.

"We should go home," Gemma said. "Get out of this place and forget the competition."

Susan blinked and showed the first sign that she'd heard any of our words. "No." She huffed out a breath and took a swig of the tea. "Don't even think about it," she added, her voice growing stronger.

Gemma sat in front of Susan and took her free hand. "The competition isn't important. You can stay at mine for a few days and process everything that's happened."

Susan downed the remains of her tea and shook her head again while placing the empty cup firmly on the table. "I'm fine. It's more of a shock than anything. I... I hate myself for being so selfish, but I can't help but wonder, why me? First Tanya and now Jeremy. It's like I'm cursed or something."

I bit my lip and decided not to admit the same thought had crossed my mind.

"But it's not about me," Susan continued. "It's about Jeremy, and he really did rave about those samples I sent him. I think we'd be doing him a disservice if you didn't enter the competition."

Gemma glanced at me and motioned for me to speak. It was clear she wanted me to mention the possibility that Jeremy was murdered. Instead, I perched on the arm of her chair and asked Susan how she and Jeremy had met.

"We met when I was at university in London. He was learning

the culinary arts, and I was being bored to death studying finance," she said, surprising me. I'd have put her down as more of a creative arts type of person. "We were at completely different schools, but met at a cross-campus party. We'd hit it off immediately and dated for almost four years."

Four years! "What happened?" I couldn't help but think back to the night before. It was clear they both cared a great deal about one another. "Why didn't things work out between the two of you?"

"My father died, leaving my gravely ill mother alone. Jeremy was making a name for himself as a master chef. He had a promising career ahead of him in London. He'd always craved the limelight. I couldn't ask him to give up all that and come to Wales with me, so I called things off."

"You loved him," I said, and Susan gave a sad smile.

"You still love him," Gemma added.

"In a way, but it's not the same, not after all this time. Too much life has happened between then and now. We kept in touch, but not seriously. Birthday and Christmas cards, nothing more. Not until I asked if he could find room in the competition for a talented baker I knew." She leaned forward and grasped Gemma's hands. "And that's why we need to stay. You have to take part and show the world what you can do."

"If it's that important to you, then we'll stay," Gemma said. "But there's something else you should hear first."

This time, when she gave me a pointed look, I couldn't escape revealing what I knew. "Kate McIntyre's here," I said, after clearing my throat.

"The Detective Inspector?" Susan looked confused, but before she had the chance to pepper me with questions, I ploughed ahead.

"Vanessa Brookes believes Jeremy was murdered, and from talking to Kate, she agrees."

"What?" Susan slumped back in her chair. "I am cursed," she said.

"You're not cursed," I said, but made a mental note to whip

up something to act as a counter-curse just in case. Tiger's eye is a protective stone that acts as a talisman against curses and ill wishes. I could weave a little extra protection into some stones and fashion them into a necklace or bracelet. Given Susan's faith in my remedies, I'm sure she'd wear it for peace of mind.

"Who else do you know that has two friends murdered in the space of a few months? The universe must hate me. Am I really that much of a bad person?"

"You're not a bad person," I said and gave her a tentative smile. "You're a very good person who bad things have happened to."

Susan looked at me curiously for a second. "Did you really just quote Harry Potter to me?" she asked.

"Actually, I believe Sirius Black said that," I replied.

Susan shook her head, but a little of the tension she'd held left her. After a moment, she stood and paced the room. "If Jeremy was murdered, that's even more reason to stay," she said. "You have to find the killer, just like you did the last time."

Gemma looked at me with questions blazing in her eyes. She knew about Tanya and how Susan and I had met, but we hadn't gone into too much detail about what had happened after that. It hadn't seemed necessary, and in truth, I'd wanted to put the whole thing behind me.

I sighed. "There'll be press and police," I said, more to remind myself of the dangers than anything else, "and we won't have much time."

"It will take as long as it takes," Susan said. "Fleur can take care of the shop, and I can give you anything you need." She stopped in her tracks and turned to face me. "I'll pay. Hire you as a private detective."

"Susan, you are not paying for anything. I'm just warning you that it's not going to be easy. We have no idea where to start and as soon as the competition ends, people will leave the hotel and go back to wherever they came from. We could end up with suspects scattered to all corners of the UK and beyond."

"Then there's no time to wait. Where do we start?"

I slumped on the chair Susan had vacated moments before

and sighed. "I've already spoken to Fleur and asked her to research hemlock." I raised my hand to still any questions. "Before you ask, Kate has a hunch it might be involved."

Susan shook her head and gave a wistful laugh. "Jeremy would have liked that," she said. "Not so much the getting murdered, but the idea of it being poison. He would have found a certain poetic irony in a chef being poisoned."

Gemma cleared her throat and stared at me. "You've already spoken to Fleur," she said and grinned. "Which means you planned on looking into Jeremy's murder even before Susan asked you to."

Susan flung herself on the edge of the bed. "Of course you did. It's in your nature."

I wasn't sure what that meant exactly, but decided to take it as a compliment. I smiled and bit my lip. "I'm not sure we have a choice," I said after a moment. "Vanessa Brookes has us pegged as the killers."

"What?" Gemma said, voicing a word that was fast becoming my least favourite, along with who, why, where, and when. As soon as the five Ws are involved, I can be sure that things are about to get far too interesting. Throw in the how and I might as well kiss sleep goodbye.

"Kate's dismissed her allegations," I said, without adding that she might have only dismissed them against me. She wasn't aware of Susan's past relationship with Jeremy. That thought led me to my next question. "Vanessa pointed the finger at us as she said Jeremy had been behaving oddly of late. She thought it had something to do with him coming here and that we were the only people he'd spoken to. When you spoke to him about getting Gemma into the competition, did you get a sense that anything was wrong?"

Susan pursed her lips. "Jeremy just sounded happy to hear from me," she said. "He asked if I was still good with numbers, and I asked him how his restaurants were doing in return. He was excited to learn that the hotel was so close to where I lived and was eager to catch up."

"Hm," I agreed. He'd said as much the night before. It was understandable to want to catch-up with an old love and see how they were doing, especially as they'd stayed on good terms over the years. But I couldn't help wondering if there was maybe something more Jeremy might have wanted to talk about.

CHAPTER SEVEN

All the colour flooded from Gemma's face and she looked just about fit to throw up as we entered the competition suite. Susan didn't look that much better. The surrounding crowds were full of chatter relating to Jeremy's death.

I told myself Gemma would feel better as soon as she started baking, but just in case, I sent Fleur a quick text asking her to bring something along to help. Frankincense was ideal to help with stress and negative emotions.

The room was full of people, easily three hundred all pushed to one side. The other side of the room was sealed off for the bakers. It housed eight workstations. They all faced the direction of the empty judges' table, which had three seats labelled with three different names. I had to admit to a little surprise to see Vanessa's name embossed on the back of her chair, given how she'd been a last-minute replacement.

A nice young man wearing a hotel badge identifying him as Mark checked Gemma's name off his clipboard and directed us to her workstation. "You've got ten minutes," he said to me and Susan. "After that, everyone who's not in the competition has to move to the observation area."

Gemma's workstation comprised one long counter with a large work area, a sink, and a built-in oven. On the counter was a stand mixer, a selection of bowls and measuring jugs, and a few other things you might find in a well-equipped kitchen. To the side, there was a small table on wheels. All of Gemma's store-cupboard ingredients, which included the few decorative items she'd been allowed to bring from home, were laid out. There was also a fridge and a freezer, which I assumed held the ingredients that needed to be kept cold.

When she entered, Gemma had submitted her ingredient list. To remove any unfair advantage gained by the quality of the produce used, the competition organisers arranged for its supply themselves. Today's bake was to feature choux pastry. Gemma had opted for a peach filling, complete with peach schnapps to flavour her cream and some of the fresh fruit, along with more liqueur mixed with cinnamon and nutmeg to provide additional flavour and a sunny shock of colour to the dish. I'd had the pleasure of being one of her taste testers and can definitely attest to its deliciousness. The second stage of the competition was to be a show-stopping vegetable-based cake. For that, Gemma intended to bake a parsnip and orange spiced cake. Despite this stage of the competition being moved to the next day, the ingredients for this bake were also laid out on the table, and I was pleased to see several nice fat parsnips sat between a couple of very large oranges and some walnuts.

Gemma glanced around and sighed while fidgeting. She moved from one place to the next, checking over everything and everyone. "Do you think it's going to stay this noisy throughout the competition?" she asked.

The crowd was very loud. "As soon as you're focused on the task at hand, I'm sure you'll block them out," I said.

"I guess," Gemma answered.

"You're going to be fabulous," Susan said, and patted her on the back.

Gemma yelped and jumped as if startled. Her nerves were worse than I'd thought. Fleur would never arrive in time with the frankincense, so I edged over to an area where tea and coffee supplies were laid out. Using the hot water available, I quickly made another batch of ginseng tea and told Gemma to down it. A second dose wouldn't hurt her any more than it had Susan.

"There's Vanessa," Gemma said, pointing into the crowds where the reality star talked with an older man, pausing occasionally to pose for a photograph with someone. Given the way he hugged her after she said something, I guessed him to be her father. I glanced around, looking for her ever-present bodyguard, but for the first time, he wasn't there. It irked me that she could chat and pose for pictures as if nothing had happened to Jeremy, but I berated myself for having such thoughts. Were we not doing almost the same thing? I sighed. Life goes on.

"There's Kate," Susan added, before clarifying to Gemma that Kate was the DI.

"This is such a weird situation." Gemma pulled a handkerchief from her pocket and wiped the sweat from her brow. "I never dreamed of entering a cooking competition, and to do so with a murder attached, police in the audience, and Vanessa Brookes thinking I might be involved is…"

"Beyond comprehension," Susan suggested.

"I was going to say, *bleeping* crazy, but beyond comprehension works well too." She sighed and looked at the judges' table. "What's the plan?" she asked after a few moments.

"You're going to focus on cooking the best peach cream puffs possible, and we'll mingle with the crowds and see what we can find out," I said. "We'll start by talking to Kate to see if she's learned anything new. After that, we'll introduce ourselves to the man talking to Vanessa."

"I wish I could stay with you."

"You're better served here," I said. "With you in the competition, we have a reason for sticking around."

Before we had a chance to say anything else, a buzzer sounded.

Susan and I, along with others accompanying the competitors in the baking area, were directed to leave. Susan pulled Gemma in for a quick hug and a peck on each cheek and wished her good luck. I did the same, relieved to see that after drinking the tea, she seemed a lot calmer and had ceased hopping from one foot to the other.

After we joined the crowd, we watched as, one by one, the judges were introduced. First, there was the Mayor of Newport, a balding man with thick-rimmed glasses, who looked to be around seventy-five. He wore his ceremonial chains and robes the deep colour of the Red Aventurine stone. The next judge was introduced as both Wales' National Chef of the Year and one of the Celtic Manor's very own chefs. She bowed, and I wondered which of the hotel's restaurants she cooked in. Finally, Vanessa was called to take her place at the judges' table. Anything that was said by way of introduction to her was drowned out by the cheers of the crowd. I sighed and shook my head. I never understood the whole reality TV celebrity thing, but from the noise, it was clear I was in the minority in that.

Ignoring the ruckus, I grabbed Susan by the hand and pulled her towards Kate at the very back of the room by the great double doors we'd entered through.

"Eira," Kate said as soon as we were in earshot, then added after a curious tilt of her head, "and Ms Reynolds. It's a pleasure to see you again, although I wish it were under different circumstances."

"Yes, it is unfortunate we only meet when I lose a friend."

Kate raised an eyebrow at this.

"Susan knew Mr Dancer from her time at university," I offered. "Yesterday was the first time she'd seen him in decades."

"Is that right?" Kate asked.

I scowled and huffed out a breath. "That's right. And she's very eager for you to find his…" I was about to say killer, but stopped my tongue. There were too many people within earshot, and I didn't want to create a panic and reveal the possibility of a murderer in their midst. "Have you made any progress?" I asked instead.

Kate ignored my question and focused on Susan. "Did you know Mr Dancer well?" she asked.

"A long time ago, I did, but as Eira mentioned, I haven't seen him for years."

"Did you know he was to be a judge when you booked into the hotel?"

"Of course, I did. I asked him for help with Gemma's late entry to the competition."

"Then last night wasn't the first contact you'd had with him in years."

"No one said that." Susan looked a little flummoxed. Her tone was uncertain, and her eyes blinked in rapid succession. "Look," she said, gathering herself together. "I don't know what you are implying, but Jeremy was my friend, and I would never have done a thing to see him hurt. I saw him briefly in the bar last night, but we retired to bed immediately afterwards, and I have not seen him since."

Kate stared at her. I could practically hear the cogs turning in her brain, but she was barking up the wrong tree if she thought Susan had anything to do with Jeremy's death.

"I thought you were over treating us like suspects," I said, but when she continued staring at Susan, I realised there must be something she wasn't sharing. "What are you not telling us?" I asked.

Kate turned her attention to me. "Following Ms Brookes' allegations, I took the liberty of checking your room key card as suggested."

"And you found that I stayed in my room all night."

"I did. I also found out who made your booking and checked your companions' records. Ms Reynolds entered her room less than two minutes before you entered yours." Kate paused, and I resisted rolling my eyes. If she had something to say, I really wished she'd just spit it out. "She left again a few minutes later and didn't return for a further twelve minutes. It was during this same time Mr Dancer left his suite. Given I now know you have a history with Mr Dancer," she said, turning back to Susan, "I'd very much like to know where you went."

Susan glanced at me, her cheeks reddening. "If you must know, I went to fetch ice. I wasn't feeling my best and thought some ice-cold water would help clear my head."

"I find it hard to believe it took you twelve minutes to fetch ice."

"I can't help what you choose to believe or not. I can only state what happened."

"I think it would be better if Susan had a lawyer with her the next time she speaks to you," I suggested. "Although, I would like to remind you of the last instance you believed someone guilty of murder and were proved wrong. Perhaps you should gather all your facts together before making any accusations."

Kate sighed and shook her head. "I haven't accused anyone of anything. I'm merely trying to get to the truth."

"The truth is, I went for ice," Susan said, as a sorrowful look crossed her face. "Believe me, if I'd seen Jeremy, I would have been far longer than twelve minutes. We had a lot of years to catch up on. Now, if you'll both excuse me, I'd like to powder my nose."

Susan left, pushing past the few people blocking the doorway. I debated following her to see if she was alright but decided against the idea. It was clear she wanted to be alone.

"You could learn to be a little less—"

"A little less what?" Kate said, scowling.

"I don't know." I shrugged. "Abrupt. Callous."

"It's not my job to spare anyone's feelings."

"It's not your job to show compassion to those who have lost a loved one in such a horrible manner! You know what Susan has already been through this year, losing Tanya hit her hard, and now Jeremy. She might not have seen him for years, but she still cared for him. You could try to be kinder to her. You don't always have to put on this cold-hearted front."

"You're a fine one to talk about fronts," she said and eyeballed me for a minute. "You know, you're not the person I thought you were. You're different from the way you were when we first met."

"When we first met, I'd just moved to the area, knew no one, and had discovered a body. I guess people do change when they start to feel comfortable in their surroundings when they make friends. Maybe you should try it sometime."

Without saying another word, I left Kate to her own thoughts and returned to the crowd watching the competition. A warmth flooded my chest when I spotted Gemma working with a smile on her face. I knew she'd relax as soon as she got into the swing of things.

I moved towards the wall to find a nice spot and watch for a while, and noticed a large poster detailing all the competition bakes. Another baker had opted for a peach filling, but there were the classic chocolate eclairs in the mix and some salted caramel ones. The poster also listed the bakes for tomorrow. I'd never realised how many vegetables it was possible to make a cake with. There was carrot, which I knew about, but also beetroot, green tomato, and courgette. Gemma was the only person to opt for parsnip, though.

The delicious scent of baking filled the air, and my stomach grumbled. I wondered about grabbing some food. I hadn't managed anything since my late breakfast, and the churning in my stomach told me I'd soon need to rectify that. I pulled my phone from my pocket and looked at the time. It was only 4:25. There was a little over an hour and a half before the competition would be over for the day. I'd never make it that long without something to eat.

I decided to leave the room and find Susan. She might be up for a quick coffee and cake break. Gemma knew we were mingling and trying to learn more about Jeremy, so I didn't feel too bad about leaving. Deciding to avoid another confrontation with Kate, I left the room by one of the side doors and sent Susan a quick text to see where she was. Within seconds, she responded to say she was in the reception lounge area.

I made my way there instantly, but when I arrived, I couldn't spot Susan anywhere. Before I had the chance to send another text, she appeared as if from nowhere and dragged me behind the large dividing wall towards a small bench outside of the main seating area.

"Thank goodness," she said and pulled me down, so my back was against the divider.

"Is everything okay?" I asked, given her strange behaviour.

"I've found the killer," she whispered.

CHAPTER EIGHT

"What?" I whispered back and cursed myself for using the word. "I mean, who?" *Bleep*! I might as well throw in a where, why, and when for the full set.

Susan looked around conspiratorially and poked her finger at the wall behind us. "I heard him on the phone. He mentioned Jeremy's death and things not going quite to plan."

"Are you sure that's what you heard?"

Susan rolled her eyes. "No, I made it up to sound dramatic."

I tried not to react to that. Not that I thought Susan would make up a story, just that at times, dramatic might as well be her middle name. "What did you hear exactly?"

"That's what I heard. He was on the phone. He said that Jeremy was dead, but the poisoning didn't go exactly to plan."

It was pretty damning. Although, what didn't go to plan? Jeremy was dead. If that was the goal, it seemed as though it worked pretty well to me. That's when something struck at the back of my mind. I remembered Jeremy's wine glass by the sink in his ensuite, but there was a second untouched glass on the table next to the bottle of wine. And at the bar, wasn't it Vanessa who suggested they open the bottle? I hadn't thought much of it until now, but that could mean two things. Vanessa could have brought the wine to poison Jeremy, or she could have been the intended victim herself.

"Where's the man?" I asked.

Susan pointed at the wall behind us again. I strained, but couldn't hear any voices. But that didn't mean he wasn't there. He could be sitting in silence after ending his phone call. I pulled Susan to her feet and told her to act natural. We walked around the divide and towards the lounge area. A few people who looked to be reporters with press passes around their necks entered from another area, but apart from our two groups, no one was there.

"He's gone," Susan said, stating the obvious.

I pulled her back around, away from the press, with a warning not to say anything within their earshot. "Did you get a look at him?" I surveyed the reception for security cameras. I couldn't see any, but that didn't mean they weren't there.

"I only caught a glimpse of him while passing. If I'd known he was about to confess to the murder, I would have paid more attention."

I raised my hand to stop her. "Let's not get ahead of ourselves," I said. "We have no idea how this person is involved. But we need to find Kate and tell her what we've learned."

"Can't you do that?" Susan said, understandably reluctant to speak to the Inspector again.

"I didn't hear or see him. You'll have to come with me." Susan deflated. It wasn't like her to act so insecure, but there seemed to be a lot of insecurity going around this weekend. "Kate's not that bad," I said. "She comes across as a bit cold, but she really does care, and at the moment, nothing is more important to her than finding Jeremy's killer."

"Not that she was any good at finding Tanya's."

"She would have got there in the end," I laughed, remembering how I'd beaten her to it. "The only reason I got there before her is because I was stupid enough to get captured by the killer."

"A handy twist of fate as I see it."

"A handy twist of fate that could have turned out very, very differently," I said, not bothering to add that it was sheer luck I hadn't become a victim myself.

"Fine. Let's go find *Kate*," Susan said with an emphasis on her name, which I decided to view as good. If Susan could look past the police aspect of Kate's persona and relate to her as another human being, I was sure she'd be more relaxed in talking to her. It would help the situation if Kate chose not to interrogate Susan this time. Although, given the circumstances, she might not be able to help herself.

"Do you think you can describe the man if necessary?" I asked while we walked along the corridor.

"I'd recognise him if I saw him again. I'm sure of it. But it was mostly his clothes I registered," she confessed. "He wore beige trousers and a baby blue shirt."

At her words, my mind was drawn back to the night before when I'd waited for Gemma and Susan in the lounge area. The man had been wearing beige trousers and a baby blue shirt. It couldn't have been the same person, could it? He'd seemed so nice. It was his nod that had made me relax into my surroundings a little. Although he had pushed his nose into his phone and ignored Vanessa when she had smiled at him. What if he wasn't ignoring her? What if he was hiding from her? I shook the thought from my mind. If she'd known who he was, I doubted a phone would be sufficient to hide him. Besides, it was a new day. He wouldn't have been wearing the same clothes.

We spent the next twenty minutes searching through the crowds for Kate. I debated calling her, but wasn't sure she'd answer the phone. As we walked, I prompted Susan with questions relating to the man's appearance.

"I know that he had hair," she said in a tone that suggested this was useful information. "But the colour escapes me for now. He definitely wasn't bald."

"Is there anything else you can add?" I asked, worried that even if we found Kate, we didn't have any real information to give her. Susan shook her head, and I continued scanning the crowd for both Kate and someone dressed like the mystery man.

My stomach grumbled, and I remembered my need for food. It came as something of a relief, therefore, when my phone buzzed, and Fleur announced she'd arrived.

"Let's grab a quick drink," I said, texting back and telling Fleur to meet us at the spa café. Hoping that I'd be able to grab a bite at the same time.

"I am a bit thirsty," Susan agreed.

As luck would have it, the café was quiet. I felt a pang of guilt at that. Good friends would all be watching the competitors bake. I did hope Gemma was doing well. We'd had another quick chance to see her when searching for Kate, but she'd been engrossed in her work and hadn't caught our eye. Her food was looking good, though, especially compared to some of the others. One poor soul's choux pastry looked as flat as a pancake.

Fleur was already sitting at one of the tables waiting for us. She jumped up and gave me a hug while Susan flopped down and waved over a waiter. "I'll take vodka and orange, hold the ice," she said before turning to me expectantly.

I chuckled and shook my head while taking my seat. "A coffee for me, thank you," I said, and Fleur opted for the same. The mouth-watering scent of jacket potatoes drifted in the air, but there was no time for a meal. "And a couple of packs of biscuits if you have any," I added. "cookies, ginger nuts, anything will be fine."

The waiter nodded, giving Fleur an extra meaningful look and a suggestive smile before leaving to fulfil our order.

She was incredibly beautiful. Her pixie cut highlighted her cheekbones and her makeup was perfect at accentuating her large, deep brown eyes. I didn't know how she always managed to look as though she'd just stepped out of a magazine. I'd call it the magic of youth, but I'd never pulled off such a feat in my day. She'd opted for a pair of jeans and a yellow cropped top today, but her ever-present ankle boots rounded out her look.

"I discovered a fair bit about hemlock," she said, but deciding that could wait, I stopped her and filled her in on Susan's overheard conversation.

"Do you really think he's the killer?" Fleur asked, sitting forward in her chair, and looking for all the world ready to spring out of it and hunt the man down.

"It's a possibility we can't ignore," I said while Susan sighed. "The thing that niggles is that he had to be talking to someone, which means more than one person may have been involved in Jeremy's murder."

Our conversation fell silent for a minute as the waiter returned. Susan grabbed her vodka before he'd even had the chance to lay it on the table and downed it in one swig. "I'll have another," she said and placed her empty glass on his tray.

The waiter finished serving our coffee, and I was thrilled to find four small packs of biscuits. He lingered for a moment and asked Fleur if there was anything else that she would like.

Susan huffed again, clearly impatient. "If you want her number, for goodness' sake, ask for it," she said, and the poor waiter blushed and mumbled an apology before leaving to get the second drink.

I rolled my eyes and vowed to leave a big tip to make up for the embarrassment caused. Fleur looked set to burst into laughter but restrained herself.

"You should give him your number," Susan said, while glancing back at the waiter. "He's got a cute butt, and a young woman like you should be out enjoying herself. You spend far too much time cooped up in that shop. You should go out more, find a man, have a good time." She shifted her pointed look from Fleur to me, and added, "That goes for both of you."

Fleur pursed her lips. It wasn't the first time Susan had brought this up. We'd both been at the end of one of her lectures. Fleur studied too hard. I was too cynical and untrusting of men — who could blame me after my cheating, criminal ex?

I blocked out the rest of the conversation and focused my

energy on devouring every single biscuit in the four small packs. What? I was hungry. Susan and Fleur bickered over Fleur's love life, or lack thereof.

As soon as I'd finished, I pulled out my phone to check the time. "We should make our way back to the competition," I said, noting there was only half an hour left. "They'll be onto the judging any minute." I pushed away from the table and went to the counter to pay the waiter. He looked at me shyly, but seemed grateful for his tip.

As I was about to leave, he cleared his throat and tried to hand me a piece of paper. "Could you give this to your daughter?" he asked.

I looked at him confused for a second, my mind unable to process what he meant. It was only when he tried to pull the paper back that I realised he wanted me to give his number to Fleur. I reached out and snatched it from his hand.

"Of course," I said, and quickly turned and joined the others.

A small sense of pride welled inside at the idea he thought Fleur was my daughter. She'd once told me that her father had been white and her mother black. With that family dynamic in my mind, it had never occurred to me that people might think of me as her mother, despite the fact I was old enough to be so. My pride soon flashed with a pang of guilt that I hadn't corrected his assumption.

"Everything okay?" Fleur asked as we started walking.

"Hmm, what... yes, everything's fine." I smiled and handed her the piece of paper. "Someone wanted you to have their number."

Susan nudged Fleur with her elbow and snatched the paper. "Rhys. A good solid Welsh name. Means 'enthusiasm'." She handed it back and added, "At least you know he's enthusiastic about a date with you."

Fleur looked sheepish for a second and rushed the paper into her pocket before speeding ahead.

I increased my pace to match hers. "Susan's right, you know. It wouldn't hurt for you to go out and have a good time once in a while. It's great having such an *enthusiastic*—" I cringed at my use of the word "—apprentice, but you have to live too."

"I know," Fleur said. "It's just not the right time. Not with Abby the way she is."

My heart divebombed into the pit of my stomach. I froze in my tracks and turned to look at Fleur wide-eyed. It took her a couple of seconds staring at my face to realise what she'd done. Her hand flew to her mouth, but it was too late to undo words that had already been spoken.

When bonded, a witch can call their familiar to their side whenever they are needed. The only problem was Abby still needed to learn to differentiate between a summons and Fleur simply speaking her name. There was a definite risk the little floofball would appear at the hotel within minutes, and there was no guarantee as to what form she might be in.

CHAPTER NINE

"Everything okay?" Susan asked, echoing Fleur's earlier words.

"I've just remembered that I left the oven on," Fleur said while bouncing on her feet and looking ready to dart along the corridor.

Susan brushed away her comment with her hand. "Do it all the time," she said. "It'll be fine."

"I'm sorry, Susan, we'd better check. We have a lot of combustible oils in the shop. Can you head back to the competition? I'll be there within half an hour. It'll take hardly any time at all to go to the shop and back."

Susan sighed and shook her head. "Fine, but hurry. I am not talking to that Kate woman without you."

Without another word, Fleur and I darted through the hotel, dodging people, and garnering many stares. As we ran, I focused my mind on Niles. Given Fleur's call to the little floofball, he wouldn't be able to stop her coming, but with any luck, he'd be by her side, and I'd be able to locate them. I had a brief flash of Abby running along the bank of the river in her natural cat form and gasped a sigh of relief. I'd seen through Niles' eyes, which meant that he was with her.

Just at that moment, a group of five men stepped out from a doorway in front of me. I barely managed to stop in time, but came skidding to a halt in the middle of their group.

"Excuse me," I said and tried to pass them.

One blocked my way and raised his hand. "Hold up there, love," he said and smiled. "Where are you off to in such a hurry?"

I didn't have time to deal with this, so I used my magic and pushed one of the men in the back of his knee. He buckled like a deck chair and sent his drink flying in the air. I discreetly flicked my fingers again and sent the glass careening into the man next to him. He shrieked as the cold beer covered his shirt and swung his arm back, knocking his companion in the face as he did so. Despite the calamity, the men laughed good-naturedly and started making fun of each other.

Fleur turned back, glared, and tsked at them before grabbing my hand and pulling me on.

Their laughter followed us through the reception and out the door. I came to a stop and placed my hands on my hips as soon as we were outside and stared up into the afternoon sky, panting. I blinked in the light and shielded my eyes. After spending so long indoors, it came as a shock how bright and open everything felt.

"They're both on their way," I said to Fleur as soon as I caught my breath.

"How long do we have?" she asked while bobbing on her tiptoes, her eyes wide with concern.

"Not enough." I glanced around, trying to get my bearings and figure out a plan. Beyond the drive leading up to the hotel, there was a large field and then a hedge surrounding an overflow car park. If memory served, I'd noted a copse of trees beyond that during my earlier walk. "This way," I said and darted towards the car park with Fleur in tow.

There weren't as many people outside as we'd encountered in the hotel, and I was relieved not to find any press present, something of a surprise given Jeremy's death and the competition, but I guessed the hotel had done their best to keep the number of prying eyes down to a minimum. But there were still too many. It was a minor miracle that Abby was in cat form, but if past events were anything to go by, that could change in a heartbeat.

"There, go into the trees," I instructed Fleur, although I was disappointed to see that they wouldn't provide as much cover as I would have liked. She glanced around and noted the couple walking in our direction.

I huffed out a breath. "Don't worry," I said. "I'll cause a distraction."

Fleur nodded and continued, dodging between the cars at a much swifter pace now that she wasn't holding back to wait for me.

I stood on the path. The people moved closer. I wasn't sure what I was going to do, but pulled my phone out of my pocket and acted like I was on a call. I glanced at the car parked on the slight incline in front of me and debated using my magic to draw it to me. Being run over was sure to draw attention, but knowing my luck, I'd end up miscalculating and breaking a leg. I wanted a distraction, not a trip to A&E.

The couple moved closer. Fleur's yellow top stood out, far too noticeable against the trees. I cursed and wished she wasn't wearing it. That fateful thought led me to my only viable idea. Although, the car thing was looking more appealing by the second.

My ingenious plan was to trip. Any decent person was sure to check if I was alright. That might keep them focused on me for a minute or two, but — I thought back to the men in the corridor and their echoing laughter — upping the calamity factor would keep them occupied for longer.

I put my plan into effect, and everything seemed to move in slow motion.

I stumbled, pretending to trip on my own feet. With a flick of my hand, I used my magic to hook my skirt onto the car next to me. It caught. I stopped my fall before I hit the ground but ensured that my skirt was ripped from top to bottom and torn from my body.

I squealed. Not needing to fake my horror or the blush that rose on my cheeks. I yanked at my skirt, trying to remove it from the car, but it was stuck tight. I stood with nothing on my bottom half apart from my shoes and the white knickers I'd donned on waking.

The couple were next to me in an instant, the wife offering me her jacket after seeing the ruins of my skirt. She held it in front of me.

"Hurry, Raymond," she called to her husband. "In my case, grab one of my skirts."

I was mortified and apologised profusely. "I am so sorry. I have no idea how this happened," I lied.

"Accidents happen," she said and flashed me a sympathetic smile. "Hurry," she snapped at her husband again.

"I don't know which one you want," he answered.

The woman reached across and delved her hand into the case. The first thing she pulled out was a top, so she tossed it to the side and plunged her hand in again. This time, she emerged with a pencil skirt and handed it to me. I slipped it on immediately. It didn't fit, and I had to roll the waistband to keep it from falling, but at least it covered my modesty.

"Which car is yours, dear?" the woman asked.

"None," I confessed. "I'm staying at the hotel and was just out for some fresh air."

Raymond flashed me a look that suggested he had little time for foolish women. "We should get you inside?" he said. "You can sort yourself out."

I nodded. My mind whirled. I hadn't thought this far ahead. I didn't want to risk a glance at the trees to see what was happening with Fleur and the cats, but equally, I didn't want to risk leaving the area in case I was needed.

"You've done far too much to help me already," I said and yanked at my skirt that was still stuck on the car. It made another tearing sound. The rags that remained of my skirt would be insufficient for me to tie them around my waist. "I can't possibly keep you any longer. If you're comfortable giving me your details, I would really like to have your skirt cleaned and returned to you along with a thank you gift."

"No gift necessary," the woman said.

"No need for cleaning. We can all go inside, and you can change," Raymond insisted.

I gasped in a deep breath of air while the couple stared at me intently. A lump formed in my throat, and I was close to outright panic. After a moment, the woman nodded and gave me their details.

"Thank you." I clutched her hand and shook it.

She nodded and dragged the man away by the arm.

He must have protested, as he turned and pointed back to the hotel. "We should just go back. For goodness' sake, it would take less than five minutes to change," he said.

"Sshh," the woman hissed. "She's obviously embarrassed and we're compounding it. Let's leave her be."

I watched as they got in their car and pulled away, giving them an awkward wave as they passed me. Only after they were no longer in view did I turn my attention back to the trees. Fleur was nowhere to be seen.

CHAPTER TEN

I connected with Niles and opened my mind to see through his eyes. An image of Fleur holding Abby flashed through my mind. She cradled the cat tight to her chest and nuzzled her head, but her eyes were wide and unblinking, staring at something on the ground. Niles turned away from them and focused on the same thing Fleur was looking at. I gasped, broke the connection, and rushed to join them amongst the trees.

"We'd better call the police," Fleur said as soon as I reached her. She looked panicked, like a rabbit caught in headlights.

Dead bodies were becoming far too frequent a part of my life, but even I had to confess to shock at seeing the man in the baby blue shirt on the ground with a knife in his chest.

I pulled my phone out, ready to call Kate, but hesitated for a moment. "Niles," I said, turning my attention to my loyal black familiar. "I need you to take Abby home. Abby, you have to go with Niles."

Fleur nodded, kissed Abby on the head, and placed the little floofball on the ground. "She understands the seriousness of the situation," she said, her eyes never leaving the body.

"Good girl, Abby. If we need you, Fleur will call. For now, it's best you're not seen."

The two cats slipped through the trees on their silent paws. I waited until they were out of view before lifting my phone. I dialled Kate. To my relief, she answered.

It had to be less than five minutes before the Detective Inspector arrived, but it seemed like more. I'd moved Fleur away from the body as she couldn't stop staring at it and then called out to the man, just in case his spirit lingered.

"Are you still here?" I asked, feeling a little silly speaking into the trees, and hoping a ghost would answer. "I need you to tell me who killed you." I didn't add that learning how he was involved in Jeremy's death would also be a big help.

The leaves rustled in the breeze and a twig fell to the ground, but no ghost emerged. Typical.

"Eira," Kate called. I turned to her voice and spotted her walking through the car park. I waved her over and pointed at the body. She sighed and glanced around, taking in our surroundings, before resting her eyes on my face. "What were you doing out here?" she asked. "It's a little off the beaten path."

"We were out for some fresh air," I lied, something I was having to do far too often.

Kate looked at the oversized skirt I'd forgotten I was wearing, despite the fact I'd only donned it a few minutes before. She raised a questioning eyebrow.

"It's a long story and not related to the discovery. There is something you should know, though. Susan and I had been trying to find you before Fleur arrived. Susan overheard someone dressed the same as this man discussing Jeremy's murder on the phone. He said something about the poisoning not going to plan."

"Jeremy Dancer's manager, Peter Falkland, has arrived at the hotel. I was talking with him," Kate said by way of explanation of her whereabouts. "Where is Ms Reynolds?" she added.

I nodded back towards the hotel. "Shall I call her? She'll be able to confirm if this was definitely the man she saw or not." I made a quick call to Susan when Kate agreed and turned my attention back to the body. "I've seen this man before," I added. "When Jeremy and Vanessa first arrived at the hotel, he was in the lounge area on his phone. I didn't think anything of it at the time, but when Vanessa walked by him, he buried his face in his phone. There's a possibility she might know who he is."

Kate nodded again and asked us to wait a few feet away while she made a couple of calls herself. She stood over the body with her back to us, speaking into the phone, relaying events, and directing others. No doubt the police would arrive in force within a few minutes.

"Are you okay?" I asked Fleur, who'd remained unusually quiet since the discovery. She opened and closed her mouth a few times, but nothing came out. "First time seeing a dead body?" I asked, and she nodded. I wished I could say the same, but this was now my third since arriving in Caerleon a few months ago. I pulled her in for a hug, unable to think of any words of comfort. Until now, I think she'd looked at the killings as an exciting puzzle to solve. Seeing the body had brought the human element back into the matter.

"We have to find who did this," she said and pulled out of our hug.

"We will," I said, and hoped that wasn't another lie. "Maybe, you should go inside," I suggested, but as I turned to lead her away, Susan came into view in the car park. "Kate," I called and nodded to the new arrival.

We moved towards her just as a police car pulled up. Within minutes, everything became a flurry of activity. Susan confirmed that the man was the one she heard on the telephone and the police started processing the scene.

"What happens now?" she asked Kate. "Surely, they'll have to cancel the competition after this second murder."

"I don't see that happening." Kate shook her head. "You should all head back inside. I'll call you if I need you."

We left and headed straight back to the competition. We'd

missed the judging and found a mass exodus leaving the competition hall. Gemma was nowhere to be seen. We decided to head back up to our rooms to see if she was there, and turned to leave.

"Eira, Susan!" Gemma's voice carried through the hubbub.

We turned towards the shout and saw her bustling through the throng towards us. Everyone was eager to hear how she'd done in the competition, but she brushed away our questions and suggested we go somewhere. We went straight to my room. As soon as we entered, Susan was on the phone ordering room service. Gemma flopped on the bed and insisted we fill her in on what we'd learnt. We told her everything. Her eyes widened and all the colour flushed from her face. I worried everything was getting a bit too much for her to cope with.

"How did the competition go?" Fleur asked.

Gemma gave a half-hearted smile, rubbed her arm, and said that her pastry had been placed in the top three. But the judges weren't divulging the order.

"That's amazing," I said. "You should be really pleased."

"I think the quality of the ingredients played a big part in bringing out the flavours. The organisers have gone for great produce. I'll have to find out who their supplier is."

Susan rolled her eyes and shook her head but didn't waste her breath in complimenting Gemma. We all knew that the ingredients could only take you so far. It was the skill of the chef that put everything together and made it perfect.

"Are you all set for tomorrow?" I asked.

"Yes. I had a little time to sort through my ingredients when we wrapped up. Everything has been laid out and still looks fresh. The parsnip's a little misshapen, but it's nice and firm, and you often get misshapen food when choosing good quality, organic ingredients. Only the supermarket cares for every fruit and vegetable to look identical to its neighbour." Gemma rubbed at her arm again and huffed out a deep breath. "It just doesn't seem that important, given everything that's happened."

"Nonsense." Susan rested a gentle hand on her shoulder. "It's tragic that Jeremy and this other man are dead, but we still have to live our lives. Besides, as much as I once knew Jeremy, I can't help but think he must have been involved in something nefarious to get killed, and this second man even more so."

She sat on the edge of the bed next to Gemma, and I took the chair opposite Fleur.

"What do we know?" Fleur asked. "You mentioned the man on the phone, but are there any other leads?"

I shook my head. "We don't know anything."

"That's not true," Susan said. "We know that the wine was poisoned, and that things didn't go to plan according to the phone call."

I sighed. "I've been thinking about that and what it could mean."

"Do you think Jeremy wasn't the intended victim?" Susan flung herself back on the bed and stared at the ceiling. "It would be just like him to be accidentally murdered."

"The thought had crossed my mind," I confessed. "There were two wine glasses. Vanessa could have been the intended target. What did the man on the phone say exactly?"

Susan sighed, and I was sure she was sick of saying the same thing over and over. "Jeremy was dead and that the poisoning didn't go exactly to plan," she said.

"In that order?" Fleur asked, sitting forward in her chair, and looking thoughtful.

"Yes, Why?"

"If Jeremy wasn't the intended victim, wouldn't things have been phrased the other way around? Sort of 'things didn't go to plan - uh-oh, we killed Jeremy by mistake'. The other way around, it's more like, 'yay, we succeeded in killing Jeremy but...'"

I looked at her clever face. "I think you might be on to something there," I agreed. "But I wonder what it was that went wrong."

Gemma scoffed. "Something that annoyed someone enough, they decided to kill the messenger."

"Could they have been looking for something?" Fleur asked.

"Something they didn't find."

"The room hadn't been ransacked."

"Unless someone cleaned up."

I thought of the spotless glass next to the sink. It certainly looked as though it had been rinsed out, but if someone had cleaned up, why not remove the glasses and the bottle of wine altogether?

"That is strange," Fleur agreed when I mentioned it, but her voice was distant, as if she was preoccupied with other thoughts.

I followed her gaze and noted Gemma was rubbing her arm again. Without saying a word, Fleur leapt from her chair and rushed towards Gemma. She knelt and pushed up Gemma's shirt sleeve.

Gemma yelped in surprise. Susan sat up in the bed and stared, wondering what was going on. She snatched Gemma's arm from Fleur.

"What the *bleep* happened to you?" she asked.

Gemma's arm was red raw, and a small blister had formed. "It's probably just nerves," she said. "I often get sensitive skin."

Fleur shook her head. "Uh-uh, no way. This is a reaction to hemlock. I read about it earlier. Don't worry. Hemlock's only poisonous if ingested, but a rash can happen with contact. It's not common, but does happen."

Gemma snatched her arm away from Susan. "It can't be. I've never been near hemlock in my life." Her watery eyes darted to Susan, and her mouth opened and closed. "I-I didn't—"

Susan clasped onto her hand and squeezed it tightly. "Oh, my dear," she said. "Of course, you had nothing to do with Jeremy's death. No one here would ever think such a thing of you."

Gemma gave her a weak smile.

Fleur jumped to her feet. "The parsnip. You mentioned it looked strange. What if it's hemlock? The roots can easily be mistaken for wild parsnip."

I joined Fleur on her feet. "I think we need to get a look at your ingredients," I said, and winced at the sores on Gemma's arm. "But first we need to clean and dress that arm."

~

Ten minutes later, we found ourselves arguing with a hotel employee named Justin, who point-blank refused to allow us entry into the storage area where the ingredients were being kept.

"You're more than welcome to come with us," I said, hoping to allay his suspicion that we were out to sabotage other bakers.

"Not a chance," Justin answered while puffing out his chest.

I cursed, huffed out a breath, and pulled the others to the side. "The only way we're getting in there is with a police escort."

"Are you sure that's a good idea?" Susan asked.

I wasn't sure at all. The last thing I wanted was to get Kate involved. Gemma had entertained the possibility we might think her capable of Jeremy's murder. Given the way things were going, finding hemlock amongst her ingredients was bound to create questions, but what choice did we have?

I called Kate, who answered her phone on the first ring. "Not another body," she said.

"No. But we think we might have found some hemlock. We're trying to get into the food storage area, but the guard is having none of it. Are you free to come and take a look?"

The line went quiet for a few seconds, but eventually, Kate agreed when I told her about the rash on Gemma's arm and the research Fleur completed.

She arrived within minutes, and after flashing her badge, Justin agreed to allow us inside with an escort, but wasn't prepared to leave his post unguarded. We had to wait for him to radio another hotel employee to take his station.

"It's over here," Gemma said as soon as we entered the room. The small, wheeled table we'd seen at the beginning of the competition was at the end of a row of eight. As soon as we reached it, Gemma rushed forward to lift the possible hemlock.

Fleur grabbed her hand to stop her. "I don't think that's a good idea," she said.

Gemma shrank back, her face white. "Sorry. I wasn't thinking."

"Are you sure this is hemlock?" Kate asked.

Fleur nodded. The root was the same cream colour of parsnip, and of a similar shape, but very skinny, especially compared to the ones on Gemma's table at the start of the day, which I recalled being nice and fat.

"They're the ones that were here when I left," Gemma said when I mentioned they were different.

"Someone must have switched them out for the parsnips. The question is, when?" Fleur said.

At this point, Justin puffed up and shook his head. "No one has been in or out of this room since it closed five minutes after the end of the competition. The door was locked, and I was stationed outside."

Susan brushed his comment away. "Yes. Yes. But for Gemma to be exposed, they had to be switched before then."

"I was working next to the table during the competition. No one came near it."

"If they have indeed been swapped," Kate said with a hint of scepticism in her voice, "there had to have been a time when the table was left alone and not locked in this room."

Gemma shrugged. "All the contestants moved to stand before the judges' table when they were tasting our bakes," she said. "After that, there were a few minutes when they let viewers back into the work area to congratulate those who did well."

I looked at my feet and cleared my throat, feeling guilty that we hadn't been there to congratulate Gemma.

"Okay," Kate said, and turned her attention to Justin. "I need to speak to the competition organisers. Everything's going to have to be confiscated."

"Everything?" Justin rubbed the back of his neck and glanced up and down the rows of tables, all laid out with the ingredients needed for tomorrow.

"We can't risk anything else being contaminated," she said. "Someone could be poisoned."

Someone already had been, but that did bring up the possibility that the killer was out for another victim. Either that or they were trying to set us up.

"It's probably just parsnip," he answered and scowled at us. From his exasperated sigh, it was clear he thought we were a group of meddlesome women, causing trouble, but he knew better than to argue with the police.

Once again, Kate made a few calls, and so did Justin. We were relegated to the side. During one call, Kate turned her back to us. I couldn't see her lips, but from the tension in her shoulders, it was clear the call added to our bad news.

"I'll get the ingredients tested to confirm whether it's hemlock," Kate said when she returned. She motioned for the others to stay where they were and pulled me to the side. When she was sure we were out of earshot, she added, "You know, this could mean one of two things."

I nodded, glad that we were thinking along the same lines. "Either someone was hoping the cake was made, which could leave the judges poisoned, or someone's trying to frame us. Both possibilities point towards Vanessa." She was the only one who knew about our involvement. She also could have been a second intended victim for the wine.

"Officer Johnson has been looking for Vanessa Brookes since you discovered the last body. So far, he's had no luck. No one has seen her since the end of today's judging."

I frowned. "Not even her father or her security detail?"

"No one. I'm going to have every spare officer on the lookout for her. If you see her, call me immediately."

"Of course," I agreed before being dismissed.

CHAPTER ELEVEN

"What did Kate say?" Fleur asked as we left the storage room.

The competition organisers had arrived and were making a fuss about their loss of ingredients, so Kate thought it best we made ourselves scarce.

"Vanessa Brookes might be missing," I said. I didn't like the woman, but I hoped she had just run off to be alone somewhere.

"Do you really think the parsnips are hemlock?" Gemma asked, as if she hadn't heard our conversation.

Susan patted her on the arm and pulled her in for a hug. "The Detective did say she would get them tested, but I think it's a foregone conclusion."

"I just... I just," Gemma swallowed and shook her head. "I can't get my head around what might have happened if I'd baked the hemlock into a cake."

"Nothing good," Fleur confirmed.

"Are we working on the assumption that Vanessa is also a

target of the killer?" Susan asked.

"I've been thinking about that, and something doesn't sit right with me." The door to the elevator opened in front of us and we entered. Gemma pressed the button for our floor, and I allowed the doors to close whilst sorting through my thoughts before continuing. "The man in the baby blue shirt was stabbed. If we're looking at the same killer, why would they poison Jeremy, stab the man, and then try to poison Vanessa along with every other judge? It doesn't make any sense."

Susan rubbed her head. "I could do with a drink."

I agreed. So much for my relaxing break. The elevator opened on our floor, and Susan suggested we all go to her room and order room service.

"I'll meet you there in about ten minutes. Order me a gin and tonic, please." I looked down at the borrowed skirt I still wore. I'd had more than a couple of funny looks as we'd passed people, and even though no one else would see me in Susan's room, I'd feel more comfortable if I changed.

I entered my room and shut the door behind me. I closed my eyes and sagged against it, enjoying the moment's silence. It had been a crazy day, and I didn't see it improving. What I really needed was another massage, or even better, a full night's sleep. I sighed. A quick shower would have to suffice. I pushed away from the door and turned to the right to go directly into my ensuite when I felt a movement in the room behind me. Before I had a chance to react, a hand landed over my mouth.

"I'm not going to hurt you," a man's voice said. "Don't scream. I just want to talk."

I readied my magic and was about to fling my assailant across the room when he released my mouth and stepped away from me.

I drew in a deep breath and decided it wouldn't hurt to hear what he had to say; flinging him against the wall was still an option if necessary. There was no doubt in my mind this was related to the murders, and he might be able to provide some answers. It's not as though I had anything else to go on.

I turned, and the man raised his hands as if in surrender. He was younger than I expected from his deep voice. Mid-twenties, maybe a little older. His almost black hair was cropped tight to his head and his blue eyes watched me intently. I realised I'd seen him before. He was the bodyguard who acted as Vanessa's shadow, but this time he was dressed in jeans and a T-shirt that stretched tight against the muscles on his chest and arms.

"Are you Eira Snow?" he asked.

"I am."

"Let's sit?" he suggested.

I nodded and hoped my nerves would keep my legs steady long enough for me to reach one of the two chairs on the other side of the room. They did. Just. "What is it you want?" I asked and sagged into the chair.

"Vanessa's missing," he said, drawing his eyebrows together. "I saw you talking to the police officer in Jeremy's room. I wanna know how you're involved." He sat forward in his chair and clenched his fists. The tension poured off him in waves. He seemed more than a mere bodyguard.

"You love her," I said as realisation struck.

"We love each other," he answered.

"Then why was she with Jeremy?"

He leaned back in his chair and rubbed the back of his neck. "We didn't mean it to happen. We just fell in love. It happens."

I frowned. Vanessa wasn't going up in my estimation. "It doesn't happen if you love the person you're in a relationship with," I snapped, thinking how easy it was for my ex to cheat on me.

"It ain't like that. Jeremy and Vanessa weren't together in a real sense. It was all for show." He sat forward and clasped his hands on his knees. "Don't get me wrong. They cared for each other, but it was to advance their careers. Jeremy was getting older and needed to make himself relevant to a younger crowd. Vanessa wanted the validation someone with his reputation gave her. It's one thing being a food blogger, but she doesn't have the weight of experience in the kitchen behind her the way Jeremy does... did. He was really helping her. They were looking into the possibility of new management. And it wasn't just her career. He was helping her learn more about running her own investments and finances, too."

"A food blogger. I thought she was a reality TV star."

The man shrugged. "Well, yeah, but reality stars have real jobs too, you know."

I didn't, but I guessed that was me told. I huffed out a breath and sat back in my chair. "For a start, I think introductions might be in order. You already know I'm Eira."

"Stephen."

"It's nice to meet you, Stephen," I said. "Although I think our meeting might have been better had you not broken into my room and held me hostage." It was an exaggeration. He hadn't, at any point, insinuated that I wasn't free to leave, but I think it hammered my point across.

Stephen had the decency to look a little embarrassed at my admonishment and apologised. "I didn't wanna risk anyone seeing us together," he said.

"Well..." I cleared my throat, straightened my borrowed skirt, and frowned, thinking. "Vanessa was never in the room with Jeremy, was she?" I asked as it occurred to me he'd referred to it as only Jeremy's room.

Stephen shook his head. "She stayed with me," he confirmed.

I nodded, not quite sure what all of this meant. "I think you'd better tell me what happened that night," I suggested.

"After we left the bar. The three of us went to his room. Vanessa had a few words with Jeremy about him being seen hugging your friend. She was worried about the optics. It wouldn't do for Jeremy to be photographed with another woman." I motioned for him to continue, but he licked his lips and wrung his hands. I could see he was on edge and wanted to bolt, as if nothing was more important to him than finding Vanessa, and he'd come to the conclusion he was wasting time talking to me.

"Cup of tea," I suggested in an effort to keep him seated. The longer he talked, the more chance I had of learning something.

"I don't do caffeine," he said.

"That's okay, I have some ginseng tea with me." I brewed us both a cup, giving Stephen time to gather his thoughts. "What happened after that?" I asked and handed the cup over before sitting opposite him with my own.

"Nothing. Jeremy apologised. Said he'd be careful in the future. They both knew their act wouldn't go on much longer. He said he wanted to go out for some fresh air to clear his head. That he'd see us both in the morning. We all left after that."

"What about the wine? The bottle of red on the table," I added when Stephen gave me a blank stare over the rim of his cup. "Was it there when you left?"

He scrunched his face, his eyes drifted up and to the left as if he was trying to remember. "Yeah, actually, it was. Vanessa opened it and poured a glass as soon as she entered the room. She gave it to Jeremy, but he put it on the table."

"She didn't touch it herself?"

"Nah. Vanessa hates alcohol. She's teetotal. Never touches the stuff."

My mind tried to process this new information. If someone close to Vanessa had wanted to poison her, it was highly likely they would have known this fact.

"Do you drink?" I asked. He shook his head.

That settled it. The poison was meant for Jeremy and Jeremy alone. That still left me with the question of how Vanessa was involved, and what hadn't gone to plan. As far as I could tell, she had no reason to poison him, but... Stephen might have. He seemed genuinely troubled by her disappearance, but I wasn't the best judge of character, especially where men were concerned. Everything he was saying could be a lie designed to get me to spill what I knew, which wasn't a lot.

I grumbled inside and put my cup down, keeping one eye trained fully on him as he finished the remains of his tea and placed his own cup on the side table next to mine. If he so much as looked at me funny, I'd have no choice but to use my magic.

"What about Vanessa's father?" I asked. We still hadn't managed to speak to him. I wondered if Kate had before adding,

"Does he know their relationship was fake?"

Stephen scoffed. "Of course he does. Was his idea. He is her manager, as well as her father."

"Then he also knows about you and Vanessa."

Stephen shook his head at this and wrung his hands again. This time, a muscle in his neck twitched, and he looked like he might punch a hole in the wall. He stood. I jumped to my feet and raised my hands, ready to blast him back into the chair with my magic. He looked at me and raised his own hands in surrender again, obviously sensing my unease.

"Sorry," he said and retook his seat. "I didn't mean to spook you." He took a deep breath and grumbled. "Vanessa made me stay well clear when her dad was around. He wouldn't like the idea of her mixing with the help. That's why I wasn't with her at the competition. That's the only reason she's missing," he added.

I picked up my tea, took a sip, and shot him another question. "Do you have any idea who murdered Jeremy?" He shook his head. "Did Vanessa?"

"She thought it was you and your friends." He looked at me, his eyes intent. Something threatening shone behind them, and I realised that was why he was here. It wasn't that he'd seen me with Kate and was trying to find out what I knew. He was trying to suss me out. If I was involved in Jeremy's death, then it stood to reason I had something to do with Vanessa's disappearance.

"I'm not involved in Vanessa's disappearance or Jeremy's death," I said, making sure to look him directly in the eyes.

His brow furrowed. He didn't seem inclined to believe me. "Why were you in the room with the Detective?"

"Kate, the detective, she's a friend of mine," I said, stretching the truth a little. "She believes hemlock might have been involved in Jeremy's death and wanted my opinion."

"Why?"

"Essential oils are a speciality of mine." I raised my hand to stop his next question. "Before you suggest anything, I'll tell you the same thing I told her. Hemlock essential oil and hemlock poison are two different things. You can look it up on the internet if you don't believe me."

Stephen sat forward in his chair, and I found myself holding my breath, waiting to see what he would do. Although I would use my magic to defend myself if need be, the last thing I wanted was to reveal my skills to Stephen, but the look on his face set my stomach churning.

I swallowed hard. "Did you kill the man in the baby blue shirt?" I asked, deciding to set him on edge.

Stephen's eyes darted toward mine. He jumped to his feet. "I ain't killed no one," he said.

I stood slowly and took a step back. Stephen glanced around the room as if looking for answers before staring at the floor.

"A man was found just over an hour ago with a knife in his chest. The police have reason to believe he was involved in Jeremy's murder." I took another step away from him.

He looked up. "I ain't killed no one," he said again, his voice barely above a whisper.

A knock sounded at the door, and Gemma called out, "You coming?"

We froze, staring at each other, then Stephen took a step forward and lifted his finger to point at my face. "If I find out you're involved—"

"I'm not."

He growled. "What about your friend? Did she steal from Jeremy?"

"Steal? What's missing?"

Before he had the chance to answer, Gemma opened my door and popped her head in. Stephen barrelled towards her. I called out a warning. Gemma squeaked in surprise. Stephen pushed past, knocking her to the ground, and continued along the corridor at full speed. I rushed towards Gemma and pulled her from the ground.

"Are you hurt?" I asked.

"Are you?" she countered, looking me up and down. "Should we call the police?"

I brushed away her comment — Kate could wait — and looked

at my skirt. "I'll fill you in over drinks," I said, "but first, let me take two seconds to change." A shower would have to wait.

CHAPTER TWELVE

Twenty minutes later, I stared out of Susan's window with a gin and tonic in hand. The sun had set, and only the bright lights of the hotel lit the surrounding area in a soft orange and yellow glow. It had shocked everyone to learn my room had been violated, and even Susan was starting to feel as though we should call it quits and head home.

"Although it's important to find Jeremy's killer," Susan said, "I don't want to lose any other friends in the process." She flopped on her back on the bed and lifted her empty glass above her head. "I'm out of alcohol," she declared.

"We could order a proper room service," Gemma suggested. "I'm starving."

My belly rumbled in response. The one gin had made me feel a little lightheaded. I hadn't had anything since the packets of biscuits and no one else had managed that. "Let's go down to one of the restaurants. It might be better for us to be out amongst people." We wouldn't get anywhere close to finding the killer or

Vanessa cooped up in Susan's room. "I don't think Stephen would hurt us," I added as an afterthought.

"He broke into your room and knocked poor Gemma to the ground," Susan protested while staring at her empty glass as if vodka would magically reappear inside it.

"Yes," I agreed, sipping the last of my gin, "but he didn't hurt us. I honestly think his main concern is for Vanessa's wellbeing."

"It would be useful to know what he thinks we might have stolen," Fleur added, as if reading my mind. She bobbed on her toes. "Where shall we eat? I hear this place has six restaurants."

"Let's do something different," Gemma said and stood from her chair. "I hear Pad in the Manor House has some delicious Asian food."

"Asian sounds good," Fleur agreed.

"As long as they serve vodka, I'm happy to eat anything," Susan added. Gemma laughed and pulled her from the bed.

We trundled as a group to the elevator and down to the reception. Banter returned, and Susan ribbed Fleur about calling the waiter Rhys.

Gemma joined in. "Call him," she said, and Fleur rolled her eyes. "No, seriously. At least one good thing might come out of this weekend."

"Two good things," Susan said, and nudged Gemma with her elbow. "Tomorrow, you're going to win this competition."

Gemma blushed and looked at her feet. "I don't know about that."

After a quick walk outside, we found the Manor House and Pad. The restaurant and lighting were stunning. Everything had a warm beige and gold feel to it, like a Fire Quartz. Most of the guests appeared to be couples on romantic dates, which meant a large circular booth was available for us to occupy. And the smells... wow! Ginger and spices. My mouth watered. If the food tasted half as good, we were in for a treat.

We took our seats, and Susan went straight to the drinks menu. "Ooh, cocktails. We'll all try a Cucumber Wasabi Martini and a Dragonfruit Mojito to start with. Four of each, please," she said to our server. Gemma tried to protest, but Susan wouldn't have it. "How often do we get to go to a cocktail bar?" she asked.

"I don't think I've drunk this much since my early twenties," Gemma said with a naughty look on her face. I had to agree. Although, in truth, I didn't think I'd ever drunk as much as I had this weekend and there was still some time to go.

"We'll go on a month's cleanse starting Monday," Susan said, and turned her attention to the food menu. "Eira can whip something up to help us detox."

"Lemon and Lavender would be good," Fleur looked at me expectantly.

I smiled. "They'd be great. Grapefruit might be good too," I suggested.

"See!" Susan smiled over the edge of the menu. "We have a plan. Now, on to food. Three courses are the way to go."

We laughed, but I think all of us were starving and up for as many courses of food as possible this evening.

As we were apparently starting a cleanse on Monday, I indulged myself and had everything fried. I ordered chilli fried squid for starters, pan-fried stone bass for my main, along with a side of wok fried asian greens, with garlic and soy sauce, and for dessert, a passion fruit delice. Everything was amazing. I think my mouth will water just thinking about the meal for months to come.

We ate our food and chatted for almost two hours. By the end, we had drunk nowhere near as much as we had the night before, despite doing a pretty good job of working our way through all the cocktails.

"I'm ready for bed," Fleur said as she stood and stretched. "I'd better get back to the flat. The cats will be hungry." She bade us all a goodnight and said that she'd see us tomorrow.

I stifled a yawn and sat back in my chair after seeing her into a taxi. Every inch of my body screamed for sleep. "I think I'm ready to call it a night myself," I confessed.

"Me too. The second stage of the competition starts at 10:30, and it would be nice if we could all grab breakfast together before that." Gemma pushed the remains of her glass away and looked at us expectantly.

"Lightweights," Susan said and stood. "Give me five minutes to powder my nose and then we can head back to our rooms." She walked through the restaurant on slightly unsteady feet, and I smiled.

I'd never imagined Susan becoming such a good friend when we'd first met. Gemma neither. I hated that I kept my true nature as a witch from them, but couldn't risk too many people finding out. Besides, we were still at the beginning of our friendships, and I didn't want to scare them away. I scoffed at that and Gemma looked at me curiously.

I brushed away her concerns. "This weekend has just been so bizarre." I reached for the jug of water on the table. After Gemma refused any, I emptied the last of the contents into my own glass. "How are you coping?" I asked, as if I was a seasoned professional who dealt with murder and kidnapping every other week. I wasn't a detective like Kate. But I had some experience, and if being a witch taught me anything, it's how to deal with the unknown.

Gemma sat forward as I drank. "I'm okay," she said. "I just keep wondering if we should still be here. I'm not sure I want to continue with the competition. If it wasn't for Susan..."

I reached across, grabbed her hand, and gave it a sympathetic squeeze. "Have you spoken to Lee or Sam?" I asked, referencing her husband and teenage daughter. They'd wanted to come to the competition, but Gemma insisted Lee stay to run the café and that Sam should help him out. In truth, I think she was more worried about disappointing them should she lose and hadn't wanted them around in case of that eventuality. Susan had highlighted all the additional praise and prestige the café would earn should Gemma win, but she hadn't taken any consideration into how it might affect business should she lose.

"Only briefly," Gemma confessed. "I gave them a quick call this morning and then again when what's-his-name... Stephen was in your room."

"What do they think about everything?"

"I didn't tell them. They know Jeremy's dead. How could they not? It's all over the news. But I never mentioned that he was murdered. Lee would have me home in a heartbeat if he knew there was a killer on the loose."

I gave her hand another reassuring squeeze and sighed. It must be nice to have a family at home who cared so much about you. I tried to think if I'd ever had that. I'd always been the one left at home, waiting, and Chris had never seemed that happy to see me for the brief periods he returned. I was nothing more than a meal ticket to him.

Still, it didn't do to sit and feel sorry for myself. If I thought about it, I was finally happy, even with all the crazy. I had Fleur, and I had friends.

My eyes drifted shut and the noise in the restaurant faded into the background. I must have dozed as the next thing I knew the server was standing next to me loudly clearing his throat.

"Excuse me, Ma'am," he said.

I sat bolt upright and prayed I wasn't drooling. I resisted licking my lips or wiping the edge of my mouth to find out and instead shot a look at Gemma. From the befuddled look on her face, it was clear she'd fallen asleep too. I glanced around and noticed that the restaurant was almost empty.

"We're just waiting for our friend," I said, wondering where Susan could have gotten to.

"Ma'am, we're about to close."

"What?" Gemma asked.

"We're about to close," he repeated. "Might I suggest you wait in the bar area?"

I pulled out my phone and looked at the time. "11:35," I said to Gemma. "Didn't Fleur leave at nine?"

"That's the time the taxi was booked for."

I shot out of my seat and cursed. Susan hadn't been enthusiastic about calling it a night, but I didn't think she'd ditch us.

We gathered our things and asked the waiter where the ladies' room was. When we arrived, we found it empty. It had been almost two hours, so that wasn't a shock, but it was something we had to check.

I tried her mobile, but it went straight through to voicemail.

"Maybe she's gone back to her room," Gemma suggested.

I nodded noncommittally. "Do you think she might be in one of the bars? Maybe talking to the bartender she saw last night."

"It might be worth a look. I just can't imagine she'd leave us," Gemma said, echoing my thoughts.

A well of dread opened in my stomach, and the more we searched and failed to find Susan, the bigger it got.

CHAPTER THIRTEEN

"Kate."

"What's wrong?" she asked, guessing that something must have happened from the sound of my voice.

"Susan's missing. We've searched everywhere, but she's gone. You have to find her. Could I have been wrong? Could Stephen have taken her? You could find out what room he's in. He could be keeping her there." The words tumbled from my mouth as I spoke without a filter.

"Okay, Eira. Slow down and start at the beginning. Susan's missing. I've got that, but who is Stephen?"

I took a deep breath and tried to gather my thoughts. Gemma sat on the edge of her bed and stared at me wide-eyed as I paced the room. She'd wanted to call her husband and form a search party. It took some doing on my part to convince her that might not be the best idea. Not that I didn't want to tear the place apart myself. I just worried that if we went anywhere with all guns blazing, then we'd seal Susan's fate. "Stephen is Vanessa's lover.

He's one of her bodyguards. He broke into my room earlier today. I think he was hoping I'd know how to find her. He thought Susan might have stolen something from Jeremy—"

"What was stolen?" Kate asked.

My shoulders slumped. "I thought you'd know," I answered while a nagging voice inside my head insisted that if we had whatever it was that was missing, then all the pieces of the puzzle would fall into place. "Didn't Vanessa mention something was missing?"

"She didn't." Kate grumbled something under her breath before returning to the call. "Where are you?" she asked.

"I'm with Gemma in her room. It's... uh..." I looked at Gemma for help as my mind drew a blank.

"Room 402," she confirmed, and I relayed the information to Kate.

"Okay. Stay where you are and stay together. It'll take me about twenty minutes to reach you, but I'm going to call Officer Johnson. He's still on site."

I ended the call and sat on the bed next to Gemma. "Cup of tea," she offered, and I knew she wanted to keep busy.

"As long as it's not ginseng," I said. I'd had enough of that particular brew to last a lifetime. It took every ounce of restraint I had not to go down to reception and slam a few hotel employees against the wall until they gave me the location of every single member of Vanessa and Jeremy's party. Not to mention her dad, and Jeremy's manager, come to think of it.

I stood from the bed and twiddled my fingers while pacing the room again, unable to sit still. "Do you think I should call Fleur?" I asked.

Gemma shook her head. "It's like you said. There's no use worrying everyone else when we don't know what's going on ourselves."

A knock sounded at the door, and I rushed to open it. "Officer Johnson," I said and ushered him in. For the first time, I was seeing him out of uniform and yet he still managed to look like a policeman with his shirt buttoned all the way up, his plain black trousers with a perfect crease down the front, and his impossibly straight posture.

"Ms Snow." He bowed his head to me. "The DI called and asked me to come and make sure you're okay and that you stay in this room."

My nostrils flared. "She said what?" He looked at his feet and a pang of guilt welled in my stomach. I grumbled it out of existence. I didn't like to be the kind of person who shoots the messenger, but sometimes it can't be helped. "You shouldn't be here watching us. You should be out there looking for our friend. Isn't that your job?"

"Ma'am—"

"Don't you Ma'am me."

Gemma grasped my arm and pulled me away from Johnson. "Eira. Sit and drink." She said it in a mummy tone that brooked no argument. I sat and took the cup as she held it in front of me. "Can I offer you a cup of tea or coffee, Officer?" she asked.

"No, Ma'am." He cleared his throat and had the decency to look a little remorseful at the situation. "I'm fine."

"We're supposed to stay here and do nothing?" I grumbled, wondering if calling Gemma's husband might not be a bad idea after all.

Gemma sat and sipped at her tea. With nothing else to do, I did the same, vowing to give Kate just ten more minutes before leaving to search again myself, and there was nothing Officer Johnson could do to stop me.

The seconds ticked by and my anger grew. I'd been stupid to get involved. Fleur had said as much, although the press had been the least of our problems. They'd been practically non-existent. Still. I'd been doubly stupid not to call Kate immediately after finding Stephen in my room. At least then, Susan would have been safe.

I thought back to the agitated young man and pictured him sitting in the chair opposite mine, sipping at his tea in much the same way Gemma did. I'd always been a bad judge of character, but was I wrong about him then or am I wrong about him now?

"He never once tried to hurt me."

Only when Johnson said, "Sorry, ma'am," did I realise I'd spoken the words out loud.

"The man who broke into my room," I said, more to sort things through for myself than to tell Gemma and Johnson what I was thinking. I took another sip of tea and sat back in the chair. Now that I'd stopped pacing and working myself into a frenzy, my heartbeat had returned to a more acceptable rate, and my mind had shifted into overdrive. "He was concerned about Vanessa. Would he really take Susan to try to find her?"

"I've not much experience in this sort of thing," Gemma said and gave me a weak smile, "But I really hope we don't have two kidnappers on our hands. Wouldn't it be more logical to think they were taken by the same person?"

"Then again, two murderers, why not two kidnappers?" I scoffed, but suspected Gemma was right.

"Two?" Kate asked, having arrived in the room without me noticing. I jumped to my feet, but she waved me down. "I know you like your secrets, but I think it's time you told me everything."

I resisted rolling my eyes. Everything! Not a chance. I wasn't about to tell her I was a witch, and that Niles was the panther she was so desperate to find, but maybe it was time to share what little we knew in relation to Jeremy's death.

We went over everything I'd learnt from Stephen: Jeremy and Vanessa not being a real couple, the fact that he thought we might have taken something, and his surprise at learning about the second dead body. I also shared the fact that Vanessa didn't drink alcohol, so she couldn't have been a target for the wine.

"Then why was the parsnip replaced with hemlock?" Gemma asked.

"I don't think anyone intended for the cake to be made tomorrow." My mind churned. I was onto something. I just wished I knew what it was. "I mean, imagine what would have happened if the Mayor, the chef, and a reality TV star had been poisoned. All right under the watchful gaze of the police. The pressure to find the killer would be immense. No. I think it was put there to make us look guilty."

Gemma shuddered. "Uh, it doesn't bear thinking about what might have happened." She stood from the edge of the bed and poured herself a glass of water. "No one but Vanessa and Stephen knew we had even the slightest involvement with Jeremy," she added after taking a sip. "That brings us right back to them as the main suspects."

"That's true. But we're working on the assumption that whoever planted the hemlock was trying to frame us in particular." I thought back to the competition hall, and the bakes listed on the poster. "You were the only entrant using parsnip. Parsnips were the only vegetables that could have been switched with hemlock without it being immediately obvious."

Kate stretched on the chair and glanced at Officer Johnson, but contributed nothing to the conversation. It wasn't the first time I'd seen her sit back and watch to see how events would unfold, and I wondered if that was part of her process: to sit back and allow people to talk themselves into trouble.

I scowled and moved to look out the window. Darkness peppered with a sprinkling of lights greeted me. I resisted checking the time, not wanting to know how long we did or didn't have until morning, how long Susan had been missing. "It all comes down to whatever was stolen," I said, without turning to look for a reaction.

"We've no way of knowing what that is," Gemma said, and I could hear the exasperation in her voice.

I closed my eyes and considered the possibility of using non-violent magical means to find Susan. Only once had I worked a spell to find a lost item. Instinctively, my hand flew to touch my right ring finger. It was bare, the ring I was reaching for was safely locked away at home. I'd worn my mother's ring for years, but it only takes one slip up to lose something forever. I'd used a chalcopyrite crystal to find it. It cleared my mind and allowed me to focus on the exact moment the ring had disappeared. I'd been too preoccupied to notice it fall from my finger when it happened, but my body retained the sense memory of the event.

I shook my head. No such memory remained of Susan's

disappearance. I opened my eyes, huffed out a deep breath, and returned to the chair.

"Has there been a ransom request?" I asked Kate. "Maybe the plan was to kidnap Vanessa all along and Jeremy was killed to keep him out of the way."

"Or to show the kidnapper meant business," Gemma added.

Kate closed her eyes and rubbed her face. "Okay," she said, shaking her head and standing. "This sounds like it might make for an interesting plot for a movie, but there's nothing to suggest anything you say is true. This Stephen could be our killer."

"Then why didn't he kill me?"

"Everything Stephen said could be a lie. Vanessa could have been dating Jeremy, the way the world thinks. There might not be any missing object. For all we know, he and Vanessa could have killed Jeremy together." I opened my mouth to speak, but Kate raised her hand to stop me and continued, "My point is, it's easy to make up wild stories to fit a narrative. We have to look at the facts and find the truth."

"And what are the facts?" I asked and let out a deep sigh. My head hurt. I was tired and a little hungover, but most of all, I was worried. I didn't want to admit it, but Kate was right. We had nothing but stories.

"Fact One," Gemma said. "Jeremy was poisoned with hemlock." Her brow furrowed, and she looked at Kate. "Or was he? There can't have been anything on the news about his murder or my husband would have called to inform me."

"The place would also be swarming with press," I added.

"Jeremy was murdered with hemlock," Kate confirmed. "I received confirmation a little over an hour ago. It was also in the wine bottle, as suspected, and the parsnip was no parsnip."

"Then that's fact two," Gemma said, referring to her switched ingredients.

"Fact three, Susan overheard the dead man on the phone. From what he said, he had to be involved in Jeremy's death."

"Fact four," Officer Johnson joined in. "That man was stabbed to death."

"Fact five. Vanessa and Susan are missing. I think that's all we know for sure," Gemma finished.

Kate cleared her throat and shook her head. "Except, fact five isn't a fact. We can't find Vanessa or Susan, but that doesn't mean they're missing. At least not in any legal sense."

I shot to my feet. "You're not even looking for her, are you?" I said, unable to keep the anger from my voice.

"We're doing everything we can to find *both* of them," she replied, emphasising the word 'both'. "But there's only so much we can do. We don't have a lot to go on."

I walked to the door and opened it. "Thank you for your time," I said. "Should we hear anything, we're sure to be in touch."

"Eira."

"Detective Inspector. I'd like the courtesy of a call should you hear anything. Now if you'll excuse us." I waved my hand through the open door.

Kate sighed and motioned with her head for Officer Johnson to leave. She followed him out the door and I pushed it shut without another word.

"What are we going to do?" Gemma asked. "There's no way I'll be able to sleep."

I debated suggesting that she call home and tell Lee everything that had happened, but one look at her face told me she'd never leave with him. "How about a cup of my revitalising ginseng tea?" I said instead, even though it was the last thing I wanted. "And then we'll change and make our way to the clubhouse bar. It doesn't close until four. Jeremy and Vanessa had a large group with them. Who knows? Maybe we'll be lucky and see one or two out for a drink."

CHAPTER FOURTEEN

"Where are you two going?" Officer Johnson asked as soon as we stepped out of the room.

I should have guessed Kate would station him at our door. "Unless you have a reason to keep us under house arrest, we're going to the bar," I said.

He pressed his lips together in a tight grimace and looked along the corridor and back at us. It was clear he couldn't stop us from going anywhere, and just as clear that Kate had told him to try.

I looked him up and down and tilted my head to the side in consideration. "You are more than welcome to join us," I said. "Just try not to look so much like a policeman, slouch a little, and I don't know... unbutton the collar of your shirt or something."

Officer Johnson smirked. He undid his top two buttons, pulled his shirt a little out of his trousers, and ruffled his hair. "It's the best I can do with what I'm wearing," he said.

Gemma linked her arm in his and smiled. "It'll do."

"But no alcohol. I'm still on duty."

"Don't worry. We're not going there to drink."

Officer Johnson grumbled at this. I guessed he was worried about what it meant. We led him to the lift and down to the lobby and then stepped outside into the night air on our way to the clubhouse bar. We hadn't visited this part of the hotel grounds yet, but given its distance from the main building and residences, I knew it was the only one still open. There was no guarantee we'd spot anyone, but it was worth a shot.

We walked in silence along the path. The waft of Johnson's cologne mixed with the crisp air. After a few minutes, the soft thump of music reached our ears, and then a row of lanterns lit the path leading to the bar. The thump of music increased as we got closer.

We'd failed to find the bartender Susan had spoken to last night earlier in the evening, but we spotted him now. He hadn't seen Susan, but promised to keep an eye out. We thanked him, ordered three bottles of water, and pushed through the crowd to find a high table where we could oversee everyone. We spotted one in the corner and made our way to it. Then, perched on the surrounding bar stools, we surveyed the room.

"What do you hope to achieve?" Johnson asked.

I shrugged. "We can't sit and do nothing."

"Tell us about yourself," Gemma said, and smiled at the officer. "We can't keep calling you Officer Johnson."

"It's Drew," he answered. "Drew Johnson."

"Oh, like Nancy Drew. Is that why you became a policeman, because you like solving mysteries?"

I smiled. It was nice for Gemma to be acting normal, at least for a little while. While we watched the room, we learned that Drew was the middle child of the local Deputy Chief Constable. I didn't know what that meant exactly, but it was clear his mother's position was high up. His elder sister was also in the force, and he stated with some certainty that his younger brother would also join. He'd studied for a Professional Policing degree at Sunderland, which included on-the-job training. He'd only come back to Wales ten months ago after a position became available for Gwent Police.

"Isn't it hard working for your mum?" Gemma asked.

Drew gave her a lopsided smile. "I don't have anything to do with her most days," and chuckled at the confused look on Gemma's face. "Think of it like working for the Royal Family. A retail assistant working at Windsor Castle might work for the Queen, but they probably never see her."

"Are you comparing your mum to the Queen?" Gemma asked and laughed when Drew blushed. "We have a fancy one here," she said to me. "We should see about hooking him up with your Fleur." This caused him to blush even more.

We sat, chatted, and nursed our water for a good hour. Our visit to the bar proved to be a lost cause. I never saw a single face I recognised as working for Jeremy, Vanessa, or her father, and I didn't have the faintest idea what Jeremy's manager looked like. He could be sitting at the next table for all I knew.

I sighed and excused myself. A visit to the ladies' room was in order. After that, Gemma definitely needed to get some sleep. She'd decided against finishing the competition, but if... no, when Susan turned up, she'd clip us both around the ears if Gemma didn't compete. I wasn't sure what I was going to do. If I could get Drew to stay and guard Gemma's door, I contemplated the possibility of popping home. Talking things through with Fleur, Niles, and Abby might help. I might even be able to experiment with a spell to find Susan.

When I came out of the restroom, I glanced around. Gemma waved from across the bar, and I stepped towards her, but froze. Stephen was going through the exit on the opposite side of the room to Gemma and Drew. He popped his head back into the bar for a second, as if searching for someone, and then left.

I waved frantically at Gemma and pointed in the direction of the door. Without waiting to see if she'd follow, I dived among the crowds, pushing through to follow Stephen.

"Ms Snow." I heard Drew call above the music, but didn't turn back. Stephen was my only chance at answers, at finding Susan.

My heart raced. I pushed outside beneath the night sky.

Stephen was nowhere to be seen, but he had to be headed back to the hotel. I raced along the path, cursing my ballet pumps. I thought I caught a glimpse of him beyond the glare of the lanterns, but couldn't be certain.

"Eira, wait," Gemma called from behind.

"Stephen," was all I managed to say between panting gasps. I'd never been much of a runner. Why run when you can walk or ride your bike? Running was far too jarring on the knees. But I kept going.

The hotel came into view. This time, I saw him. I risked calling out to him, but couldn't muster the air to shout very loud. On impulse, I flicked my hand and used magic to push the door outwards, hoping to knock him to his feet, but I was too late. I pushed for more speed. The lobby light was blinding. I shielded my eyes and heard the distinct ping of the lift

I doubled over, wanting to cry. I'd been too late. Straightening, I walked over to the lift, not caring about the clop of my shoes as I walked. I pressed the call button. The lift continued to ascend, and then the light stopped on the fifth floor.

"Come on, come on," I said and crossed my fingers.

The light counted down, highlighting each floor as it passed. Four, three, two, one, and open. It wasn't a lot, but it was something. The lift had stopped on the fifth floor and come straight to my call. That's where Stephen got off.

I glanced back at the main entrance. Gemma and Drew still hadn't arrived. I debated waiting, but when the lift doors started to close, I pushed my hand out to stop them and stepped inside.

My heart raced. I didn't know what I was going to do, but if I had to knock on every single door on that floor until I found Stephen, so be it. All too slowly, the lift rumbled to life and carried me to my destination. I hesitated for a second when it stopped and swallowed back the lump forming in my throat.

CHAPTER FIFTEEN

I couldn't say why I felt so nervous stepping from the elevator. Maybe I knew that if I didn't find Stephen in the hallway, I'd have to knock on doors. I'd have to use my magic. Not that I didn't have faith in my abilities. It was being exposed that I worried about most of all. If people found out what I could do, I'd have to sell the shop and move away. That was the last thing I wanted.

Despite the warmth of the evening, a sudden chill shook my bones. The hallway bent away from me in two different directions. I looked right and then left, debating which way to choose, even though I knew deep down it didn't matter. I sighed, straightened my back, and opted to go left. The only sound that followed me along the bright open corridor was the soft thud of my feet on the carpet and the gentle hiss of my breath.

I shook my head and tried to chase away the chill creeping up my spine. I was looking for someone. That was all. So why did my skin itch, and my heart race as if something was about to happen?

I walked slowly, making sure to pause at every door, listening for voices. At times, I heard the rumble of a TV or the gentle hum of someone snoring. But nothing that would help me identify the occupants.

I sighed, rubbed my head, and decided to give the corridor to the right a try. I made my way back towards the elevator and was about to round the bend when the faint squeak of a door sounded behind me. I rushed forward, pressed myself against the wall out of view, and steadied myself. I peeked around the corner. The fifth door back on the left opened, and Vanessa's father emerged from its shadow.

I flung myself against the wall, not sure what to do. I debated calling the lift and acting natural. As far as I could tell, he was alone. Maybe if we got in the elevator together, I could speak to him without the possibility of his or Vanessa's security interfering.

His footsteps sounded nearer, and I told myself to calm down. He rounded the corner. He was older than he looked from a distance. In his late sixties. He must have been around my age when Vanessa was born. I turned to smile at him in that awkward way strangers have when they cross paths. He smiled back, and I focused my attention on the elevator doors. He stepped up beside me and leaned down.

"Eira Snow, I believe," he said as if my name was a threat. I turned to face him and stepped back, not liking his closeness. He gave me a wry smile.

"Have we met?" I asked, even though I knew we hadn't.

"No," he answered. "I'm Stan Brookes. Vanessa is my daughter. I believe you already know that. My employee mentioned you were following him." He ran his hand over his slicked-back hair and grabbed my arm. I tried to shrug off his hand, but he gripped me tighter. "It's time we talked."

He pulled me back along the corridor to the open room. I let him, half hoping to find Susan inside. I kept my head low. He pushed me inside and slammed the door.

The light came on, illuminating the room. I was in a suite

remarkably similar to the one Jeremy had been staying in. Stephen sat on one of the plush sofas. Another man stood by the window.

"Sit." Vanessa's father pushed me to the sofa opposite Stephen. I sat, glaring at Vanessa's lover. It was only then that I noticed the tension he held in his shoulders and the worry etched around his eyes, and realisation struck. He was dreading what would happen if I said anything about his relationship with Vanessa.

The whole situation suddenly became very... bothersome to me. I'd been dragged into a stranger's room and was now surrounded by three burly men. Not one of them knew I was a witch and could hold my own, and the thought that they intended to bully an isolated woman quite rightly had my back up.

"Where's Susan?" I demanded, my voice strong, and my eyes never leaving Stephen's face.

"Where's my daughter?" Stan countered and sat on the sofa next to Stephen.

I shifted my gaze to him. "I don't know where your daughter is," I said and asked again after Susan.

"I'm not a patient man, Ms Snow. I'll ask you one more time. Where is my daughter?"

"And I will tell you one more time. I. Don't. Know."

He nodded to the man standing in the corner, who stepped forward and cracked his knuckles. "Perhaps Derek can change your mind," he said.

I narrowed my eyes. A part of me really wanted to see how far they would take their act of intimidation and threat of violence, but another suspected it was no threat. I hadn't taken a particular liking to Vanessa, but I completely despised her father.

Derek smiled and moved closer. I resisted standing, but held my breath, waiting to see how close he would get and if I'd have to act. I wouldn't get answers if things escalated into a fight. An image of Niles flashed through my mind. He reached out to see if I needed help. I must have been sending him some mixed signals. I sent him a message to say I was fine, took a deep breath, and vowed to get my emotions under control before his instincts had him charging to my rescue.

Derek was almost on top of me. He cracked his knuckles again and rolled his shoulders.

"I'm missing a friend. You're missing a daughter and," I added while looking at Stephen, "I also believe something was taken from Jeremy."

Derek looked at Vanessa's father, who raised his hand to stop him from advancing any further. "What do you know about Jeremy's watch?" he asked.

My mind whirled. Jeremy's watch! The one Susan had given him? I tried to process this new information but couldn't make sense of why the watch could be the key to everything, and why did the tone of Stan's voice make me believe he cared more about the watch than he did his daughter? "I don't know anything about its whereabouts, if that's what you're asking. I'm just wondering why you think I might know where your daughter is when it's more logical to think that the same person took both Vanessa and Susan."

He looked at me curiously and rubbed his chin. I held his gaze and after a while, a smile flashed across his face. "Stephen here said you weren't involved," he said, as if he'd come to the same conclusion. "But I had to be sure. You understand." He nodded to Derek again, and the goon returned to stand by the window. Stan stood. "I think I like you, Ms Snow. Can I offer you a drink?"

"No. Thank you." A tension I hadn't realised I'd been holding flooded from my body. If Stan was prepared to be more courteous, maybe there was a chance I could get answers, after all. I took a deep breath. "Do you know why Vanessa and Susan might have been taken?" I asked.

Stan continued walking to a side table where a decanter was laid out. His back stayed to me, and he didn't say a word. He poured himself a whiskey. I stood and took one step towards him.

"Hey," Derek edged forward.

Stan turned and lifted his hand. "It's perfectly fine, Derek." He leaned with his back against the side table and watched me over the rim of his glass as he took a sip. "I don't know why Vanessa was taken. And apart from the little information I received from my daughter and Stephen here, I know nothing of your friend Susan."

I glanced at Vanessa's boyfriend. It was clear he feared Stan, and not just because he was dating the man's daughter. Stan was a thug. I didn't know much about Jeremy, but it seemed strange to me that he would be involved with such a man. "You strike me as a man who might make enemies," I said, keeping my eyes locked with his.

He took another sip of whiskey. "Is that a threat, Ms Snow?"

"No. It's an observation." I sighed and ran my hand over my head. "If you have any idea who would kill Jeremy and kidnap Vanessa, I'd be grateful if you told me."

A slight smile played at the edge of his lips. "I would think your presence here is proof enough that I have no idea where my daughter is." He placed his now empty glass on the counter. "It seems we're both wasting our time, and that we both have people to find, so if you'll excuse me, I have calls to make and other avenues to explore."

I glanced at Stephen, who avoided my gaze, and then at Derek before moving towards the door. I reached out with my hand poised on the handle and swallowed hard.

"What does the missing watch have to do with all this?" I turned and met Stan's eyes.

"I suspect it has nothing to do with anything."

I nodded as if agreeing and opened the door. "If you find out anything, I would appreciate your sharing it with me."

"A word to the wise, Ms Snow. Stay out of this. If I find your friend, I'll let you know. But keep meddling, and you could attract the wrong kind of attention." He smiled, but the threat in his words was clear. "Not everyone's as nice as I am," he added.

I stepped out into the hallway and shut the door, along with my eyes. After taking a deep breath, I decided to go back to Gemma's room and make sure she was alright. After that, I'd check in on Fleur and decide my next steps. I had no doubt in my mind that Jeremy's missing watch had something to do with his death, as well as Susan and Vanessa's disappearance.

Five minutes later, I knocked on Gemma's door. "Who is it?" she asked, her voice weary.

"It's me, Eira."

"Eira." The door flung open, and Gemma pulled me in for a deep hug. "Where the *bleep* have you been?"

"I—"

"Don't you ever do that to me again!"

"I'm sorry." I pulled back. "I'm fine. I saw Stephen leaving the bar and followed him. I then ran into Vanessa's father, and we talked for a short while." From the pallor of Gemma's face, I decided to leave out the bit about him practically kidnapping me. "The good news is, he's working on finding both Vanessa and Susan, so for now, I think we both need to get some rest." I walked her inside her room and glanced at the clock. It was nearing 2 am. "I have a good feeling about things," I said to reassure her, then noticing Drew's absence, asked where he was.

"He told me to stay right here while he went looking for you. I have his number. I'd better call him and let him know you're back."

I smiled. "Tell him I'm going straight to bed and not to worry. We'll see him in the morning. And then get some rest." After one final good night, I left the room and returned to my own.

I had no intention of calling it a night, but neither Gemma nor Drew needed to know that.

Only after I'd passed the door to my ensuite did I sense the presence of someone inside. I didn't have the chance to turn before a heavy blow glanced my head. Not again, I thought as an explosion of light flashed behind my eyes and I crumpled to the ground as blackness overtook my consciousness.

CHAPTER SIXTEEN

"Eira. Eira, wake up."

I winced at the pain in my head and debated the possibility of a spell that would protect it from future injury. At the rate my brain was being knocked about these last few months, I'd be lucky not to suffer permanent damage. I opened my eyes to Susan's worried face.

"I'm okay," I said, relieved to see that Susan was too. I glanced around the room. From the furnishing and layout, we were still in the hotel and in a room similar to mine. Vanessa sat on one of the chairs while Susan and I were on the sofa. Her eyes were puffy, as if she'd been crying. "Your father's looking for you," I said.

She turned her attention to the four thugs surrounding us. "See. You'd better let me go. As soon as my dad finds you, you're going to regret ever laying a finger on me." The venom in her voice was tinged with worry, and I realised just how young Vanessa was. She may be a couple of years older than Fleur, but life had dealt the two women vastly different hands. Where Fleur had been forced by circumstance to mature quickly, Vanessa had the privilege of staying young in the protective bubble of those around her.

"Don't worry," I whispered to Susan. "I'll get us out of here."

"I know you will," she said and smiled.

I glanced around the room. The heavy curtains were drawn, and the only light came from the central bulb. It would be simple enough to take it out with my magic. Two lampshades stood on side tables. I could use them as projectiles. Let's see how these guys like having something bashed over their heads. The man who currently used a knife to pick under his fingernails would be my first target. The one leering at Vanessa could be my second. That left two more. Thankfully, I wouldn't need a weapon to take them out. A simple push would have them falling over into each other. I wouldn't even need the power in my Melody Stone to help.

Susan looked at me quizzically, and I got the impression she'd read into some of what I planned. She bit her lip and looked set to bolt as soon as I told her to. But if I acted now, and we fled the room, our captors would have the chance to regroup and escape before the police could arrive. And we'd be no closer to finding out what on Earth was going on. Knowing he was on his way, I flashed Niles a message to stay back, but be ready should I need him. He sent me back an image of him, standing with Abby and Fleur in the copse where we'd discovered the body. Fleur looked resolved and as ready to fight as the cats. No doubt Niles had filled Abby in and, in turn, the white floofball had told Fleur.

"Why are you after the watch?" I asked, deciding to come right out and ask the burning question. The only reason for our captors to keep us alive was if they were searching for something they hadn't found. That had to be the watch.

The man sporting a T-shirt that was two sizes too small and with a tattoo of a snake on his arm moved towards me and smirked. "Then you admit you have it," he said. "The boss will be pleased." As he said the words, his mobile phone rang in his pocket. He pulled it out and answered it. "I think we might finally have the lady we were looking for," he said and handed the phone to me.

I looked at it dumbfounded for a moment, and he motioned for me to take it. "Hello," I said, feeling foolish.

"Ms Snow, I hope you understand the seriousness of your situation."

The man with the tattoo had moved around to the back of the sofa as the man on the phone talked. He yanked Susan back by her hair and placed a gun against her head. I dropped the phone, worried that I'd ruined everything with my need for answers. If I'd acted moments ago and used my magic the way I'd planned, Susan would be safe.

"Pick it up," the man with the gun said, motioning towards the phone.

I glared at him and returned to the call. "What do you want?" I demanded.

"I want the watch."

"Is it really worth killing for?" I asked.

"Are you willing to find out?"

"I don't have the watch," I said.

"Liar," Vanessa screamed and jumped forward, looking as though she was ready to scratch my eyes out. The man who'd been leering at her pulled her back down into the chair. "I saw Jeremy showing it to you. She," she spat at Susan, "had it in her hand. I saw you take it."

"If you saw us take it, why didn't you tell the police?" I snapped.

Vanessa glared at me. "Daddy said—"

"Shut up," the man on the phone shouted, while my mind processed the new information. Vanessa may have been cut off, but I suspected she was about to say that Stan had told her not to tell the police about the watch. "Just tell me where it is," he continued.

"Susan gave the watch to Jeremy as a present years ago," I said. "What you saw was friends reminiscing. We didn't take the watch." I thought back to the night we talked to Jeremy in the bar. What had he said? I hadn't noted it at the time, but he'd mentioned that the situation would have to be pretty dire for him to part with his pocket watch. A strange thing to say. Unless it was a coded message. Unless he knew he was in danger and planned on passing the watch to Susan. But he hadn't. I'd watched as he put it back in his pocket. And with that realisation I suddenly knew exactly where it was. "It must have been quite a shock to murder Mr Dancer and find the watch missing," I said into the phone.

"I'm sure it was for whoever killed Jeremy," the man on the other end of the line answered.

"I don't have the watch, but I know where it is," I responded. "Let me get it and exchange it for my friends."

"A deal I'd be more than happy to make. All I want is the watch."

"Why should I trust you?" I asked and shifted my gaze from the gun at Susan's head to the man still prying under his fingernails with a knife. "You say you didn't kill Mr Dancer, but what about the other man, the one in the baby-blue shirt who was stabbed in the chest?"

The man on the phone laughed. "He wasn't someone you should care about. Believe me when I say he got what he deserved."

"Then you admit you killed him."

"I admit I had him killed. Which is why you should trust me when I say that I didn't kill Jeremy, and I won't kill you if you give me what I want."

"Where can we meet to make the exchange?" I asked, hoping I was right about its location.

"There's no need for that. My men can accompany you. As soon as they have the watch in their possession, they can call, and I will give the word for our other guests to leave unharmed."

"No. That's—"

"I'm sure you can understand that this is the only way things are going to play out, Ms Snow," he said, and told me to give the phone back to his man.

The gun remained glued to Susan's head while the tattooed man talked on the phone to his boss. He nodded a few times, even though the caller couldn't see him, and then pocketed the phone when the call ended. "You two," he said, and motioned to the leering goon and one of the others. "Blindfold her."

I stood. "How am I supposed to know where I'm going if I can't see," I said.

"You'll be able to see fine as soon as you're well away from this room. Don't try any funny business. It would be a shame to have to kill anyone."

One of the men placed a pillowcase over my head and bound that around the eyes with something. "Everything's going to be fine," I said to Susan, my voice muffled.

"I know," she answered. "I trust you."

I felt a pang of guilt at her words. I would do everything I could to save her, and I would save her. But she had no reason to trust me, not when I kept the secret that I was a witch from her.

Someone guided me across the room and opened the door. I reached my hand out and stopped myself on the door frame before walking through. I needed to know something before I left. "It was nice of your father to give you a bottle of wine for Jeremy," I said, being sure to be loud enough for Vanessa to hear me.

"What?" Vanessa said, the tone of her voice relaying her confusion. "It was Jeremy's favourite. A thank you gift from Daddy for all the help Jeremy's been giving me."

Susan gasped, knowing what that meant. Ever since I'd spoken to Stan, I'd had a nagging thought eating away at the back of my mind. It might have been nothing more than a father's focus on his daughter, but Vanessa had confirmed it wasn't. When I'd asked him if he knew who might kill Jeremy and kidnap his daughter, he'd only confirmed that he had no idea where his daughter was. He'd also asked me about the watch and Vanessa's whereabouts, but never once did he suspect me of being involved in Jeremy's death. Add to that the fact he hadn't wanted the police to know the watch was missing… all the pieces fit together.

Whatever else was said was cut off when I was shoved out the door. It slammed behind me, and one of the men spun me around on the spot a few times before leading me down the corridor. We walked, taking twists and turns and doubling back on ourselves a few times to ensure I would completely lose my bearings. When they finally removed my blindfold, we were in the underground car park.

"It's your turn to lead the way," the man who carried the knife said.

It was easy to find my room from the car park. It's where Susan had parked when we'd first come to the hotel. We took the lift to my floor, and I led the men to my room.

"I've already searched this room," the man said as I opened the door and entered, leaving the room in darkness. Thanks to my connection with Niles, my night vision was as good as that of a cat. I needed only one-sixth of the light a normal human does.

"Then you couldn't have searched it well enough."

He pulled his knife and pushed me against the wall. "You'd better not be trying any funny business," he said.

The blade pressed against the chain of my pendant. When I'd been kidnapped after investigating Tanya's murder, sheer anger and a good deal of luck had allowed me to blast Trisha against the wall and knock her unconscious. After that, I'd woven a spell and enhanced my abilities with the Melody Stone. Fleur and I used it to move furniture. It was time to see what else it could do.

The second man closed the door and moved to turn on the light. Before he had the chance, I channelled my power through the stone and blasted the man with the knife into him. They both fell to the floor in a huddle, and I wasted no time in calling the lamps across the room and into their heads.

They groaned, and I whacked them again for good measure before rushing across the room and finding something to tie their hands with. As soon as they were bound, I pocketed the knife-guy's phone and sent a mental message to Niles. I needed him to stay close with Abby, but to have Fleur to meet me in the lobby. Niles could relay the message to Abby, and she'd be able to pass it on to Fleur. Instead of going straight to meet her, I rushed out of the room and across the hallway to Gemma's and pounded on the door. She was up in seconds.

"Eira," she said, but I pushed past her without responding.

On the floor, amongst Gemma's recipe cards, was Susan's

unopened package. The package lying forgotten since Susan learned of Jeremy's death. I ripped it open, and sure enough, found the pocket watch inside.

"Eira, what's going on?" Gemma asked.

"Jeremy died for this," I said and turned the simple object over in my hands. "Vanessa and Susan were taken *for this*."

"For a watch? Why?"

That's what didn't make sense. It was an antique and probably cost a pretty penny, but nowhere near enough to kill for. So, what was it about the watch that made it so important?

I twirled it in my hand and flipped it onto its face. I wondered... I tried to remove the back cover, but it wouldn't budge.

"I have a pin," Gemma said, and rushed to retrieve it.

She handed it to me. I slipped it beneath the rim, being careful not to scratch the casing, and popped the cover. Inside, I found a bright violet-blue pressed periwinkle and an SD card. I left the flower in place but removed the card. "Jeremy wasn't killed for the watch," I said, and lifted the card to look at it. "But for whatever's on this."

CHAPTER SEVENTEEN

I told Gemma everything that had happened. How I'd seen Susan and Vanessa, how Vanessa's dad had supplied the wine and killed Jeremy, and how there was another player. This man had killed our man in blue and taken the hostages. And everything boiled down to this little SD card and its contents.

Gemma snatched it out of my hand. "We have to call Drew and the Detective Inspector," she said.

"And if we do that, what happens to Susan and Vanessa? No. I can't take the chance our mystery player will kill them." I huffed out a breath and worried over the time already lost. "I need you to give me an hour," I said. "Keep that card safe, and if I'm not back, call Drew and Kate. Tell them everything. Oh, and also tell them two goons are tied up in my room."

Gemma glanced nervously at the door and swallowed. "I don't know about this, Eira."

"They won't break free," I reassured her, even though guilt felt like a lead stone in my stomach. "I'm good with knots."

"Okay," she agreed after a moment. "But what are you going to do?"

I popped the casing back on the pocket watch and tossed it in the air before catching it again. "Everyone's been asking where this is. I think it's time I took it to them."

"You can't do that. It's not safe. You could be hurt."

I gave her a wry smile. "I can take care of myself," I said and mentioned that I knew martial arts to alleviate some of her worries. "How else do you think I took out the two men in my room?" I added.

Gemma sat on the edge of her bed and glanced at the wall clock. "Your hour starts now."

I huffed out a breath and rushed from the room to meet Fleur in the lobby. She jumped up from her chair as soon as she saw me arrive. "What's going on? Niles has looked set to bite someone's head off for the last hour and Abby's not been much better. They've been completely freaking me out."

"It's a long story." I grabbed her arm and pulled her towards the lift. "I'll explain on our way upstairs."

I led Fleur to Jeremy's suite. It was where everything started, and with any luck, it would be where everything ended. We didn't have a lot of time, and I wanted to catch everyone involved.

"Are you sure this is a good idea?" Fleur asked as I laid out my plan. "You could call Kate."

I sighed. I knew calling Kate was the sensible thing to do, but I also knew that Susan and Vanessa would both be dead if I did. That's not to say my plan was without risk. I was fully aware that we could all end up dead. But Fleur and I were capable of more than anyone knew, and with our Melody Stones, our abilities increased tenfold. We were our best shot at saving everyone and catching our killers.

"I'll understand if you don't want to take part," I said, and Fleur's face dropped.

"There's not a *bleeping* chance in hell you're doing this without me. I just want to make sure you think it's the right thing to do."

"Right thing? Maybe not," I said, echoing my earlier thoughts. "But it's what needs to be done."

After a nod from Fleur, I pulled the knife-guy's phone from my pocket and huffed a relieved gasp when I found it unlocked. I flicked through the numbers. When I'd spoken to our mystery man, I hadn't noted a name on the phone, but I had noted most of the number and it didn't take me long to find that same number on this phone.

I closed my eyes, running through a conversation in my head, wanting to get my words straight before making the call.

"Rob, do you have the watch?" the voice I recognised from earlier asked.

"Rob doesn't, but I do."

"Ms Snow. I'm not sure you know who you're dealing with."

"Actually, I'm not sure you know who you are dealing with." He tried to cut me off, but I snapped at him to listen. "I have the watch, and as far as I'm concerned, the deal we made still stands."

He cleared his throat and came back at me in a clipped tone. "The deal *we* made was for *you* to take *my men* to the watch."

"No. That's the one you forced on me. I said I would fetch the watch and make an exchange. Well, I'm ready and willing to make that exchange. Are you?"

He grumbled, but relented. "Tell me when and where you want to meet?"

I told him and added, "It has to be you who makes the exchange. And don't worry, I'm not stupid enough to think you'll come alone. Just make sure your men bring Susan and Vanessa with them. I'll be holding the watch out the window when you arrive. If I don't hear your voice and know it's you. I'll drop the watch to a waiting friend."

"Are you willing to see all your friends die if you do?"

"I'm willing to take the chance you'll keep us alive, knowing that you'll never see the watch again if you try anything. I guess the big question is exactly how important it is to you?"

"I'll be there," he answered and ended the call.

I sagged into the sofa and let out a gasp of air. That was one line hooked. Now to add the second. My stomach churned, but after Fleur squeezed my hand in a reassuring manner, I walked over to the room phone and lifted it before calling reception.

"I'd like to speak to Stan Brookes in suite 4, please? Yes, I understand what time it is, but Mr Brookes will want to speak with me. Tell him it's Eira Snow and that I have the watch."

The line went quiet for a few moments before Stan came on the line. "You have it," he said, his voice gruff.

"I do. And if you want it, I need you to meet with me in twenty minutes."

"Where?"

I pushed down the nausea building in my stomach. "In the place you murdered Jeremy."

Stan chuckled. "I thought I warned you not to meddle."

"Ah, yes. Your word to the wise." Word to the witch was more like it. And this witch would never abandon her friends. "Twenty minutes, Stan," I said, my confidence growing with my annoyance. I was about to hang up, but paused and added, "Oh, and not that you care, but I also found your daughter. She'll arrive at the room a little after you do."

I flopped back in the chair and closed my eyes.

"You okay?" Fleur asked.

"I'm fine." The strange thing was that was the truth. With Chris, I'd always been unsure of myself, doubted my ability to do anything. I realised now that was his conditioning of me. I wasn't useless. I could say boo to a ghost, and I didn't need to hide away. It's just a shame it took me half my life to realise that. Still, better late than never. "Okay. We'd better get ready," I said and opened my eyes.

CHAPTER EIGHTEEN

Fleur and I spent what little time we had planning. I wanted her to stay back and out of harm's way as much as possible. She was there as back-up when needed, and I'd prefer if her face was never shown.

We couldn't account for every possibility, but we could do our best to plan for the worst. The mystery man had at least two men that would come with him, and then there was Stan Brookes. He'd have Derek and probably Stephen. But both men could have others that I knew nothing about, especially considering the size of Jeremy and Vanessa's security detail when they first arrived. And I knew of at least one gun in play.

Plus, there was Drew to consider. I hadn't seen him about the hotel, but he was around. I was sure of it. If he spotted the groups of men on the move or saw Susan and Vanessa being dragged around the hotel, he might appear and throw a spanner in the works.

Finally, we needed to stage the room. I'd chosen Jeremy's suite on impulse. It was on the top floor, away from the busier parts of the hotel, and I hoped somewhere we could contain the situation. There were also three rooms, the main lounge area and the two bedrooms, which would give Fleur somewhere to hide and also somewhere I could send Susan and Vanessa to get them out of harm's way. The problem was, I hadn't really thought beyond that.

I bit my lip. Everyone had underestimated me so far. Why wouldn't they? I was a forty-one-year-old shopkeeper, with crazy hair, and a knack for getting myself into ridiculous situations. I just had to hope that underestimation would still hold. Although I didn't doubt that both groups were preparing for an ambush.

"How long do we have?" Fleur asked while bobbing on her tiptoes.

"They could be here any minute," I answered. "It's time to hide."

"Abby's going crazy, calling into my mind. I think she wants to come and help."

I smiled. "Niles is the same. But we have to keep them out of it, for now. But to be ready if and only if we call."

It must be hard on our familiars. Fleur and I were on edge, worried about what might happen. They knew that and were fighting their instincts to intervene. I had to say I was impressed with Abby. The little floofball might be a little flighty with her powers, but when it came to the crunch, she clearly understood the seriousness of the situation and would follow commands.

Fleur ran her hand over her pixie cut and edged into the bedroom on the right side of the room. She left the door open a crack and turned off the light. With her bond to Abby, her eyes were as good as mine in the dark. I mirrored the staging with the door on the left side of the room, and then turned off the main light, plunging the room into darkness. I switched on the lamp nearest the window and stood by it, ready to toss the pocket watch outside should the need arise.

"You ready, Fleur?" I asked into the darkness and clutched my Melody Stone for reassurance.

"As ready as I'll ever be."

We fell silent after that. My breath hissed in and out, my heart thundered, and I debated calling the whole thing off. Kate and the police were only a phone call away. Too many things could go wrong, and if they did, it would all be on me. The seconds ticked away, seeming more like hours, and I imagined the sound of footsteps in the hall outside the room. Those spectral noises faded into insignificance when the real thud arrived and a knock sounded at the door.

"It's open," I shouted.

CHAPTER NINETEEN

I held my breath, caught between one second and the next. The door edged open. Stan and Derek stood silhouetted by the hallway light.

"Are there just the two of you?" I asked. Stan stepped into the room. Derek a second behind. "What? No Stephen," I added.

"You're a very foolish woman, Ms Snow," Stan said while casting an assessing gaze around the suite.

"I've been called worse. Close the door. If you try anything, I'll drop the watch out the window, and you'll never get your hands on it."

Stan's gaze flicked to my hand, resting on the lip of the open window. He laughed and nodded to Derek, who closed the door. A second later, he lifted a gun, complete with silencer, and pointed it at me. "How about you give me the watch and I won't shoot you," he said, smirked, and pulled the trigger anyway. Even with the silencer, the crack of the gun was almost deafening. His aim was off and designed to scare me, but my reaction was instinctual.

I squealed and lifted my hand up before my face, sending a blast of magic outwards from my body. The force I'd channeled through my pendant to stop the bullet caused a backlash. The lamp shattered, plunging the room into complete darkness. Stan and Derek were thrown against the door, but it threw me against the wall beside the window. My arm cracked against the ledge. Pain lanced through it, and I almost dropped the watch. With my night vision, I could see that Derek was out, but Stan was on his feet in seconds. Confusion shone on his face. He couldn't know what had happened, but it was clear he rightly put the blame on me. He'd dropped his gun in the blast but stumbled around in the dark trying to find it. Fleur stepped from the side room and flicked her hand, causing the gun to skitter on the floor towards her. As soon as it reached her feet, she kicked it into the bedroom, out of reach. Stan froze, listening for a second before flailing in the direction of the thin beam of light coming from under the door.

I decided to give him a helping hand in reaching his destination and flicked my hand. All it took was a little magical nudge to send him careening into the door.

"Let's get them out of sight," I said after confirming both men were out. I never could have imagined a time in my life where I'd render a man unconscious, but here I was, standing over two prone forms. So far today, my total was four. I wondered how many more I might add to that list with the arrival of the mystery man and his goons.

I patted Fleur on the arm and gave her a smile to confirm if she was okay. She gave me a nervous smile back.

"Life's not always like this," I said to reassure her that this was far from normal. Although, who knew what the new normal was these days? Maybe Susan wasn't cursed, maybe it was me. A karmic punishment for not realising Chris was a crook sooner and saving goodness knew how many people from being conned.

Fleur and I gathered Derek and Stan up with our magic and deposited them on the floor in the ensuite. I closed the door, sealing them in, and blasted the lock to ensure they couldn't escape the room.

"That gunshot was louder than expected. Do you think anyone heard?" Fleur asked.

"Let's hope not." I rubbed at my eyes. I didn't want to admit anything to Fleur, but my arm throbbed, and a bone-deep weariness engulfed my body. With the Melody Stone, I might be able to move mountains and even stop bullets, but that came with a price. I felt like I could sleep for a week. But I had no choice but to push through. "Are you sure you can set up the phone?" I asked.

"It's easy."

"Do it while I clean up the mess from the lamp. Then we'd better get back into position." Our mystery man was due any minute, and we had to be in place for his arrival.

We didn't have to wait long. This time, no knock sounded at the door. It opened and Susan stepped inside. Behind her and with a gun pointed at her head was tattoo man. He motioned for her to enter the room. Vanessa followed behind them. Another gun rested against her head and tears streamed down her face. Finally, a man I'd never seen before entered the room. He was balding, with salt and pepper wisps of hair scattered about his head. His suit looked expensive, tailored to his large frame with a matching waistcoat. The top three buttons on his shirt were undone, and no tie completed the outfit. He flicked on the main light, and I cursed myself for not removing the bulb.

"Ms Snow," he said, and I instantly recognised his voice as that of the mystery man calling the shots on the end of the phone. He spread his hands wide. "I'm here as requested."

"Put the guns down and I'll give you the pocket watch."

He looked at me quizzically and walked towards one of the chairs before taking a seat, then rubbed at his chin as though thinking. His eyes never left my face. "I'm getting bored with games, Ms Snow. Sit down and we'll talk."

"Remove the guns from my friends' heads and we'll talk," I countered.

"I don't think so. Now sit or my men will start breaking fingers."

Vanessa whimpered. I wanted to use my power and start

blasting away, but couldn't risk the guns going off by accident. If only they'd point them in a different direction for a second, I'd have my chance. I looked from Vanessa to Susan. Susan appeared a lot calmer than anyone else in the room. She gave me an almost imperceptible nod of her head, and my heart almost broke. She still trusted me to get her out of this. What had I ever done to deserve her faith in me?

A pit formed in my stomach, but I pulled my arm from outside the window and lifted the pocket watch for the man to see. I then motioned to the cupboard on the right and the phone on top of it.

"I have your face on camera," I said and walked over to sit opposite our mystery man. I resisted sagging into the chair, though every ounce of my body begged for me to sleep. I was running on adrenaline, but even that was fading.

His calm demeanour wavered for a second. "What makes you think I won't kill you all and delete the footage?" he said, recovering his composure.

"You could try, but it's a video call hooked up to a friend of mine. She's recording the images as we speak. If anything happens, she's going to send the recording straight to the police."

In truth, we couldn't risk recording events for fear of being caught out as witches. The other end of the call was connected to Fleur in the next room. If things had gone to plan, she'd taken a screenshot of our guest's face as soon as he'd entered and emailed the image to herself. She'd tagged Kate in the body of the email. Kate wasn't a direct recipient, but would no doubt find the message should anything go wrong.

"What do you want?" he asked.

"The only thing I want is for me and my friends to get out of here safely. Let Susan and Vanessa leave, and I'll give you the watch."

"You're not the person I thought you were," he said with a pensive look on his face.

"I've been getting that a lot lately."

He sat forward and laced his fingers between his hands. His eyes bored into mine. "You're tired," he said, stating the obvious.

I gave him a weak smile. "It's been a long day, and I'm growing weary of talking. I don't think you have a lot of options here. You can take the watch and leave, or you can kill us, and my friend sends your image straight to the police. The choice is yours."

"That doesn't seem like much of a choice on the face of things." He motioned for his men to move. They pushed Susan and Vanessa down onto the sofa.

I watched their movement, ready to take action should the opportunity present itself. I just needed those guns to be pointed elsewhere. Then an idea struck me. One that just might work. I resisted smiling and sent a mental image to Niles, telling him what I needed him to do.

"Just give him the watch already!" Vanessa shrieked.

"As I said before," the man said, ignoring her outburst and focusing all his attention on me, "you're not who I thought you were. An hour ago, I'd have been happy to have my men collect the watch and release your friends, but now things are different. I suspect you know that it's not the watch that's important, but rather the contents of the watch that I'm after."

Susan frowned, and her eyes widened as if she suddenly realised that Jeremy must have hidden something inside the watch.

I could have cursed, but instead smiled. "Stan Brookes killed Jeremy Dancer for whatever's on that SD card," I said, knowing it was pointless to deny I'd found it.

Vanessa shifted in her seat. "Daddy wouldn't—"

The man raised his hand to silence her.

"I've been wondering what he could possibly possess that would be so important, and then I remembered a few things." I turned my attention to Susan. "When you spoke to Jeremy on the phone, you said that he asked if you were still good with numbers."

Susan nodded. "But that was just because I'd studied finance at university."

I smiled. "I think there was more to it than that." My focus shifted to Vanessa. "Stephen told me how Jeremy Dancer was helping you. Not just with your career, but by looking into your finances and investments, too. Stephen even mentioned the possibility of new management."

Vanessa shook her head, not wanting to process my words, but her eyes flashed to our mystery man, confirming my suspicions. "Daddy's my manager," she mumbled while staring at her hands in her lap.

"Let me guess, he also runs your finances? I hate to be the one to break it to you, but I suspect that your father's been stealing from you. He killed Jeremy to keep his secret."

Vanessa buried her head in her hands. I couldn't help but feel sorry for her. I didn't know where she came from or what life she'd led, but no one deserved to be betrayed by their own family. I knew all too well how that felt.

The mystery man gave me a slow clap. "I'll say it again. You're definitely not the person I thought you were, Ms Snow. You're very perceptive."

"Then it should come as no surprise that I know you're Peter Falkland, Jeremy's manager."

"Actually, I suppose it doesn't. What gave me away?"

"For starters, when we talked on the phone, I referred to Jeremy as Mr Dancer. You didn't echo my words. Instead, you opted to use his given name. The way someone close to him would. And then, there's your interest in the watch. Jeremy told you what he'd found, didn't he? He trusted you."

Peter sighed and shrugged his shoulders. "Jeremy was a good friend. Had he been alive, I would have honoured his wishes, but dead..." he spread his hands as if to say, 'it is what it is'. "He called me from the hotel shortly after he arrived. He mentioned seeing you and a man in the lobby. He described the man to me and said that he'd seen him somewhere before. Jeremy suspected he worked for Stan. He told me all about the files and records of Stan syphoning money from his daughter's accounts and had all the details on how to access them. He'd been foolish enough to tell Vanessa's father what he knew. He gave Stan to the end of the weekend to return the money and tell Vanessa she was free to seek new representation. I guess we all know what happened after that."

My gaze flicked to Vanessa. Her eyes were closed. Fresh tears streamed down her cheeks. Her youthful innocence had fled her features and the look that remained spoke of how deep her father had hurt her by his actions.

"I'm sorry, you had to learn about everything like this," I said, honestly wishing that Jeremy's plan had worked. Wanting to ease her suffering in any way I could, I added, "I think you should know that Stephen loves you very much. He knew about the missing watch, but he's the only one who was never interested in finding it. All he cared about was finding you safe and sound."

She opened her eyes and wiped away her tears. "There's not much chance of that," she said and glanced at Peter.

I suspected he believed she was right. Even if we gave him the SD card, we knew too much to keep alive.

"There's one more thing you should know," I said, sensing Niles had scaled the side of the building and now waited in place. "I'm not as perceptive as you may think. Jeremy told me everything. The truth of the matter is… I see dead people."

At that moment, Niles rapped on the window. Everyone turned to look for the origin of the sound. All that was visible through the black of night was a dark, shadowy presence that sucked in the surrounding light. His emerald-green eyes shone like floating lanterns.

"What the *bleep!*" Susan's tattooed captor exclaimed just before the light popped out.

Good girl, Fleur!

Vanessa screamed. Susan called out my name. Peter cursed.

I sprang into action, blasted the guns away from the men, and lifted all three from the floor, bashing their heads on the ceiling. They came crashing down.

Fleur stepped into the room and turned on one of the remaining lamps.

"Eira," Susan barrelled towards me and flung her arms around my neck.

Vanessa stood and looked about, dumbfounded. "W-what happened?" she asked. "Jeremy's ghost."

"There is no ghost," I said, as soon as Susan gave me a little breathing room. "I just needed Peter and his men to think there were so we could disarm them."

Vanessa shook her head again. The poor girl had been subjected to far too many shocks this evening. It wasn't fair of me to add more. But a made-up ghost was the least of her worries.

"This is my friend Fleur," I continued. "She cast two beams of light against the window, and I have another friend below who I asked to throw stones and make some noise outside. Fleur and I do a little bit of martial arts," I said, deciding to go with the same lie I'd given to Gemma. "With their attention focused on the fictitious ghost, we were able to turn off the lights and knock them out." I walked over and pulled Vanessa in for a hug. To my surprise, she let me.

Susan eyed me curiously, and I was left with no doubt that she knew I was lying. I just hoped she'd forgive me for it. There may come a time when I could tell her the truth, but today wasn't it.

"We'd better tie them up and call the police," Fleur said.

I nodded and pulled away from Vanessa. "Call Stephen," I told her. "I wasn't exaggerating when I said how much he cares for you."

"But Daddy—"

"The watch," Susan said, as if suddenly remembering it.

I handed it to her, and she flipped it over. "It's not easy to get off," I said, sensing she needed to see inside herself.

Susan smiled and twisted the casing a few times. "It has a knack," she said. Her hand flew over her mouth when she found the flower inside. "It was from our first date," she said. "I put it inside for Jeremy to keep."

"I wondered as much," I said, knowing from the look on Susan's face that it was right to let her see the pressed periwinkle for herself. "I took out the SD card," I added. "It's safe with Gemma."

CHAPTER TWENTY

Gemma stood in front of the judge's desk with a beaming smile on her face. The Mayor stepped forward and gave her the first-place trophy. The crowd erupted in applause.

"I'm so proud of her," Susan gushed beside me.

"Me too," I said, echoing her sentiment.

The night had flashed by in a blur of activity and, given the circumstances, the competition had yet again been postponed for a few hours for us to get some much-needed rest.

"Woohoo!" Lee whooped. "That's my wife."

"Dad." Sam flushed a bright beetroot beside him.

Speaking of beetroot, Gemma had been allowed a last-minute change to her planned recipe. She didn't think she could make a parsnip cake without worrying it was poisonous hemlock. Either way, it was delicious and took her right to the top of the competition.

Vanessa walked up to her and pulled her in for a hug. I couldn't hear what she was saying, but Gemma blushed as brightly as Sam did.

After a flurry of activity, the crowds thinned, the area was slowly cleared away, and we took our party to the café. Despite managing a few hours' sleep, I was still bone-weary and wanted nothing more than to go back to bed. Not even my ginseng tea had helped me. But no matter how exhausted I was, it was important for me to be here for my friend. Still, I made a mental note to explore the limitations of the Melody Stone. The way I felt warned of the possibility of over-exertion in its use. The human body, even that of a witch, could only take so much.

"So, you and Vanessa looked very close at the end there," Susan said, and nudged Gemma with her elbow.

"Did you get her autograph?" Sam asked, perking up and looking like she might be paying attention to our conversation and not deep into whatever was happening on her phone, after all.

"I didn't get an autograph, but as she's coming to the café tomorrow to trial our breakfast, you'll be able to ask her then."

"Oh my God! Are you serious?" Sam stood and hopped up and down in her seat. "I have to call Jessica and Bella... and Seren."

Gemma shook her head and raised a finger. "Those three and no more, and they must be sworn to secrecy. I will not have the place overrun with teenage gawkers. You hear me."

Sam squealed and rushed over to the wall to frantically call her friends.

"I'd say it was the excitement of the young," Lee said, taking a sip of his coffee, but I'm damn near buzzing myself. "Vanessa Brookes is going to write an article for the café on her blog. With her reach, it could be phenomenal for business. You should see if she'll do a piece on your store too," he added to me.

"She's a food blogger. I'm not sure she'll be interested in my crystals and oils."

"Nonsense. She could put the focus on those miracle teas you blend."

I shrugged. "You never know. It might be worth a shot."

Before I could say anything else, Kate appeared and waved me over. I sighed. She hadn't been impressed with me and Fleur going it alone last night. As well as enduring an endless barrage of questions, she also subjected me to a scolding, as if I were a two-year-old. Still, the only thing that mattered was that everyone was safe, and the bad guys were all caught.

"You look tired," she said as soon as I reached her. She motioned for me to sit at an empty table. I was grateful for the thought.

"This is a fine mess you unravelled last night," she said as she sat opposite me. "Stan Brookes has been stealing from his daughter since she started her career at thirteen. We're talking millions spent and millions stashed away. It's no wonder he didn't want anyone finding out. He would have been looking at ten years."

"I didn't unravel anything. You can thank Jeremy Dancer for that."

"Stan Brookes and his man seem at a complete loss as to how you managed to ambush them."

I sighed, not wanting to go through everything again. Apart from the fact, I hated all the lies; I was just too tired to care. What was done was done. It was time to move on.

"Peter Falkland, on the other hand, jumps at the slightest sound or shadow. He seems to think Jeremy Dancer's ghost is out to get him."

"I explained all that last night. I made up a story to distract them. There was no ghost."

"Hmm, hmm. It does seem strange. All the odd things spotted when you're around. Ghosts, panthers. I can't wait to see what the next case brings."

I scoffed. "There's not going to be a next case. It's far too exhausting."

"If you say so. Not that I'm complaining, mind. Peter Falkland's fear of Jeremy Dancer has him confessing his sins and those of his associates. The CPS is going to have a field day sifting through everything. It seems that despite his position as a celebrity manager, he moved in some very dodgy circles."

"Well, I'm glad everything worked out for you," I said.

"It did."

"Eira," I turned and spotted Fleur waving at me from down the hall. She jogged up to me and rested her hand protectively on my shoulder. "Everything okay?" she asked.

"Everything's fine," Kate said. "I was just giving Eira an update." She stood and nodded to the people sitting at the other table.

"We'll speak again soon, I'm sure."

"Til then," I said.

~

Printed in Great Britain
by Amazon